I0555892

LEARNING TO LOVE AGAIN

FINDING LOVE IN WAKETON
BOOK ONE

KELLI HENEGHAN

Published by
Kelli Heneghan

This is a work of fiction, Names, characters places and incidents either are
the product of the author's imaginations or are used fictitiously. Any
resemblance to actual persons, living or dead, events, or locales is entirely
coincidental.
All rights reserved. No part of this book may be reproduced or transmitted
in any form or by any means, electronic or mechanical, including
photocopying, recording, or by any information storage and retrieval
system, without the written permission of the Publisher, except where
permitted by law.

Copyright © 2015 by Kelli Heneghan
Edited by Nathan Squiers for Literary Dark Editing
Cover art by EmCat Designs

DEDICATION

For Doug, Duncan and Mary:
The three people I love the most in this world.

ACKNOWLEDGMENTS

I have to say Thank You to my family---my husband and kids have left me alone so I could write, edit and revise more than I probably deserve!

A huge debt of gratitude goes out to Nathan Squiers, who took a chance on an unknown and agreed to be my editor.

He would not let me get away with lazy writing, or do anything the easy way. He went above and beyond anything I had ever expected from an editor. I'm pretty sure I drove him crazy but he always had time for me.

I also owe a lot of heartfelt thanks to Megan J. Parker for an awesome cover and for agreeing to do my formatting. Not to mention all the suggestions and offers of help. You are priceless! Without you and Nathan, this would still just be a file on the computer.

To my best friend Jennie, the only person who read almost every single version of my work in progress. I couldn't have done this without you!

And to Laura and Allie and Becky—thank you for being my

Beta Readers. You have no idea how much that meant to me.

FOR ALL OF THOSE WHO
WONDER, WHAT IF I HAD A
second chance...

CHAPTER 1

T he first thing nicole was aware of was the pain. It seemed to be coming from everywhere all at once. She tried to open her eyes, managing mere slits, but the bright lights made her wince and shut them again. She heard voices talking above her. Something about the voices tugged at her memories, but the pain was too intense, she couldn't focus on them. She couldn't focus on anything. She let out a whimper.

She heard movement beside her and tried to move her hand, only to find it was held in the firm grasp of a large, calloused hand. She held on all as if this hand were her lifeline; she didn't want to be left alone. Someone leaned over her, breath warm against her ear as they whispered to her. There was too much pain, however, and she couldn't concentrate enough on the words to understand them at first. Gradually, she was able to push past the pain to listen through the haze.

"...but you're okay, now. Try to keep still, kid. You've

got a lot of tubes and wires coming out of you. Squeeze my hand if you understand."

Nicole squeezed with every bit of strength she could muster.

"That's good, kid. I knew you wouldn't quit on me. You're too damn stubborn," the voice reassured her, and she finally recognized it as her best friend, Jack Williams'. She tried to stay focused, but she felt herself drifting back into the void.

Groaning, she tried to open her eyes again. As she tried to focus on Jack's face, Nicole was thankful the room wasn't as bright as it had been before.

"What..." her throat hurt, and her voice was just a croak.

Jack reached for her hand again, giving it a gentle squeeze. "You were in an accident four days ago. They kept you under heavy sedation to keep you from moving around so you wouldn't pull out any stitches or anything. The police called the ranch, and Maria got hold of me. I've called Mitch and Carly, but they're on that cruise ship in Alaska, and Uncle Steve and Aunt Helen are still on that humanitarian mission with the church; I'm still trying to get word to them," He explained.

She swallowed hard, closing her eyes again. Her head was pounding and the lights only made it worse. Trying to take all of this in was too much of a strain. Someone said her name. She forced her eyes open, wincing at the shooting pain it caused.

"Well, Miss Winters, glad to see you have decided to rejoin us," a male voice to her right announced. "I'm Doctor Fredricks." He removed his stethoscope from around his neck. Nicole blinked her eyes, attempting to focus on her doctor. He was tall, a little overweight, thinning hair, and quite a bit older. "I'm just going to do a brief exam. Don't worry about talking too much right now. I'm sure your throat is still sore from the breathing tube."

Doctor Fredricks listened to her heart and lungs and checked her pupils and reflexes, and pulled up a chair to sit next to her. "You are one lucky young woman, Miss Winters. We've had to keep you here in the ICU for the last few days, sedated, until we could determine the extent of the injuries you sustained in the accident. Tonight, we'll try to move you up to one of the orthopedic floors, so we can start some physical therapy."

He glanced over at Jack, and Nicole followed his gaze, catching the grim look on her friend's face. "I'm not going to paint a pretty picture here for you, Miss Winters. I saw the photos of the accident. You are lucky to be alive, lucky your injuries weren't even worse. But your recovery is going to be painful. I'm not going to go into all of that right now— I can tell your concussion is causing you enough of a headache." He pushed himself to his feet, "I'm going to leave and go write some orders. I'll tell the nurses they can start introducing a clear liquid diet and then maybe tomorrow we can start soft solid foods."

As soon as the doctor left the room, Jack moved over to the doorway and dimmed the lights before moving over to sit down at the edge of her bed. "You can rest, if you need to," he reassured her, reaching out a hand and smoothing it across her forehead. Nicole let out a heavy sigh and a groan with every slight shift of her body, the ache reminding her she'd just been in an accident. A nurse entered the room and changed out the IV bag and injected something into the IV line.

"That was just a dose of pain meds. You'll be asleep soon. We'll see about moving you upstairs the next time you wake up," she told her with a smile before leaving the room.

"Have you..." Nicole had to stop to clear her throat. "Have you been here the entire time?" She studied the lines on his face, seeing they were deeper from fatigue and worry. His dark hair was tousled, and she could imagine him pushing his fingers through it over and over again during the days she'd been out.

"Pretty much. I got a hotel room down the street, but I haven't used it much." He took a deep breath. "Christ, Nicole, I thought...When the cops called—they had to use the Jaws of Life to get you out. You were trapped for close to two hours before they got to you. I didn't know what I'd be walking into when we...when *I* got here." Jack paused, clearing his throat. "Do you remember any of it?"

"Some." Nicole tried to concentrate. "I remember the rain and the headlights coming toward me." Something about what Jack just said didn't sound right, but she couldn't get her mind to wrap around it. "Everything hurts," she told him on a groan as she tried to move again.

"I don't doubt it. You're bruised pretty much head to toe, plus you had a collapsed lung, broken ribs, and you damn near broke your back." Jack told her, as he shoved his fingers through his hair.

With a slight smile, she reached over and took his hand in hers. "I'm going to be okay, though, right?" she asked, fighting to stay awake.

"Yeah. I made sure of that," Jack gave her an answering

grin, a movement outside of the door catching his eye. Turning his head to glance towards it, he frowned before refocusing on her. "Look, kiddo, now that you are awake, I think I'm going to head back to my hotel. I need a shower, decent food and a nap, and I'm not picky about which order I get them in." Trying not to touch any of her bruises, he ran his free hand over her head. And you need some rest, too. Have the nurses call me if you need anything."

"Jack," Nicole held tighter to his hand for a moment. "Thank you."

"For what?"

"Being here."

"You were there for me when I needed you. I'm just returning the favor." As her eyes drifted closed, he squeezed her hand one last time. "I'll be back later." Walking out of her room, he shut her door behind him.

JACK STEPPED into the hall and looked around, seeing the man he was looking for leaning against the nurses' station, waiting for him. Shaking his head, Jack headed towards him.

"Jason, what are you doing hanging around outside her door? What if she'd seen you just now?"

"I just needed to be sure she's okay," he glanced down the hallway towards Nicole's room. "This is not the way I wanted to get her back, forcing her to accept me as her physician. How is she?" Jason's eyes swung back to his friend.

"Hard to say right now," Jack studied his friend. "You

do realize that if she finds out that you're involved in any way with her care, she's liable to run?"

"I don't know how we can keep it from her. I'm the accepting physician in Waketon. She'll have to find that out sooner or later," he pointed out.

Jack released a ragged breath and glanced at the hospital room he'd just left before returning his attention to his friend. "I was hoping that wouldn't happen until after we get her *back* to Waketon," he muttered, shaking his head. "I just have a bad feeling that you are going to cost me one of the best friends I've had since childhood." He narrowed his gaze. "I'm warning you, you mess it up this time, and I'm not going to help you fix it."

"I will not mess it up this time," Jason growled at him.

Jack rubbed his neck and then turned towards the elevators. "I'm headed to the hotel. Call me if anything changes," he called over his shoulder, knowing his friend wouldn't be leaving the hospital anytime soon. God help them both if Nicole found out Jason was here and involved in her care, let alone he'd helped orchestrate it. She'd string them both up by their balls if she caught them. But right now, he was too exhausted to care.

CHAPTER 2

Nicole grimaced as she tried to get comfortable in the unyielding hospital bed. She'd been moved to a private room on the orthopedic rehabilitation unit the day after she'd woken up. Now, they were allowing her to get out of bed for brief periods of physical therapy. Too brief. She was bored out of her mind, lying there in the stupid thing for the past few days. There was only so much mindless TV a person could take.

Especially when that person had a headache the size of Montana and Texas combined, she grumped to herself as she turned off the TV.

She felt the tears threatening again. One of the doctors had warned her that was to be expected with head injuries, and that her emotions could be all over the place for a while. "That's just great. Between hormones and now this, I'm going to gain two-hundred pounds from eating chocolate all the time," she had griped.

"I wouldn't recommend that. The excess weight will make the recovery on your pelvis even harder." The doctor had advised, taking her comment at face value. He didn't seem to understand the concepts of sarcasm or humor.

She sighed, glancing up at the clock. Jack was late. He was usually here helping to alleviate the boredom. She knew he had some calls to make to his clients that morning; he'd told her that much the night before.

He would have called her if he'd had to return to Wake-ton, wouldn't he?

She let her head drop back onto the pillow and closed her eyes, trying to relax, and praying the headache would go away, if even just a little. Hearing the door open, she opened her eyes and looked over, expecting to see Jack or her nurse. Instead, she was surprised to see her friend Carly standing there.

"Carly! When did you get in? You shouldn't have cancelled your trip for this!" She accepted her friend's warm hug, managing to get one arm up and around her shoulders.

"Don't be silly. We saw what we wanted to see in Alaska, and you need us here. As soon as the captain could get us back to the port, so we could get the flight to Anchorage, well, that was that hard part. Anyway, Jack's been keeping me and Mitch updated over the phone, but I needed to see for myself that you're okay. How are you really doing?" Carly stepped back and put her hands on her hips, studying her friend. "Because, let me tell you, you look like crap."

"Gee, thanks, but I *am* doing much better now." Nicole brushed her fingers over the bruises on her cheek and forehead. Not brave enough to look in a mirror yet, she could tell by touch alone how big most of the bruises were. And they were all tender.

She shifted, trying yet again to find a more comfortable position. "How bad do I look?" she asked, catching her friend's eyes as Carly studied her face.

"I guess compared to what you *could* look like, you're not that bad." Carly pursed her lips. "With the right hair and make-up, we could say you're just trying to bring the punk-rock look back into style."

"Knew I could count on you to give it to me straight," she muttered, adjusting her position again. "I can't *wait* to get out of this joint. I'm so tired of being here."

Carly sat down on the edge of the bed. "Jack said they're talking about discharging you in about a week or so, as long as we get someone who can do the rehab."

"That shouldn't be a problem. I live in Austin. There are rehab places all over town," she pointed out.

"Uh, you're not staying in Austin, hon."

"Why wouldn't I stay in Austin? I live here, my apartment is here, and my life is here." *Who had the head injury here, anyway?* Nicole watched a guilty look cross Carly's face and her stomach felt as if it were tied in knots.

"All of your doctors agreed you can't live alone right now. So, you're coming back to Waketon with us. I thought they already told you all of this?" Carly wouldn't meet her gaze.

She shook her head, wincing at the pain that shot through her temples. "No. No way. I don't think so. No way in hell am I going back to Waketon. I can't go back there, Carly. I'll hire a live-in. Where is Jack, and Mitch for that matter?"

"They were talking to one of the doctors in the hall. I'll go see if they're done." Carly jumped up and bolted out of the room, glancing down the hall to the nurses' station where she'd left her husband and his cousin talking to one of the doctors and Jason.

Carly hurried to the group of men, turning to slug Jack on the arm.

"Ow, Carly! What the hell!" Jack moved away from her, rubbing his bicep.

"You told me Nicole knew she'd be coming to Wake-ton, which is something she has no desire to do!" Carly told him between clenched teeth. "She says she'll just hire a live-in and stay here."

"Over my dead body!" Jason interjected.

"Keep your voice down, Jason, before she hears you. Then we'll never get her to Waketon," Jack advised his friend, glancing down the hallway to make sure the door to Nicole's room was closed. "And Carly, calm down. The woman has a head injury, broken ribs, damn near broke her pelvis and back. I don't think she's in a position to fight us on this." He glanced at Mitch, "I told you this would be fun. You ready to go do battle with your favorite cousin?"

"Why is she only my favorite cousin when she's irritated with you and I have to fix things?" Mitch questioned with a wry grin as the two set off down the hall.

Carly glanced up at Jason and gave him a reassuring smile. "Sorry. I shouldn't have dragged you into the family drama. Thanks again for agreeing to be her doctor. I know things didn't end on a good note between the two of you and you didn't have to do this..." her voice trailed off.

"You all are still my friends, Carly. I'd do anything

for my friends," he told her, giving her a quick hug. "Listen, this will probably go a lot smoother as long as she doesn't know I'm around. Have the guys call me if anything comes up. I need to get back to Waketon." He turned and headed down the hall. Carly watched him for a second before turning and heading towards her friend's room, entering it to hear Nicole telling Mitch in no uncertain terms she had no desire to move back to Waketon.

"Nicole, your car was totaled! You can't drive yet anyway, so you have no way of getting to appointments. You live on the second floor, your apartment complex doesn't have an elevator, *and* you live alone! God forbid if you should fall or something, there's no one around to help you!" Mitch argued.

Nicole's gaze moved between the three people standing around her bed, her eyes filling with tears. Again. She was getting so sick of these emotions.

"I don't have a choice here, do I?" her voice was a whisper.

Jack sat down beside Nicole on the bed, slipping an arm around her shoulders. "Sorry, kiddo. I'm afraid not. We just don't want anything else to happen to you."

Nicole shook her head as the tears slid down her cheeks. Mitch handed his cousin a box of tissues as Carly sat down on the other side of her friend. Nicole closed her eyes, trying to get her thoughts in order.

"What about a live-in?" she asked. She watched as Jack and Mitch exchanged a look. Something was up; they weren't telling her everything. She narrowed her eyes. "What aren't they telling me?" she turned to Carly.

"What...what do you mean?" Carly's eyes went wide and she looked to her husband for help.

"There is something you three aren't telling me, and I want to know right now what it is!" Nicole wanted to push away from everyone. God, being bedridden sucked! "I'm serious, Carly, tell me right now!"

"Nicole, you need to calm down." Mitch said.

"You calm down, Mitch Williams! You're not the one who is having your entire life rearranged without your consent!" Nicole was losing what little control she had left and her voice was steadily climbing.

"Look, Nicole, they expect rehab to take a minimum of six months, maybe even longer. There's no way you can struggle with stairs and an apartment and living on your own for that long," Jack stepped between the cousins. "And you live in a one-bed room apartment, so quit with the talk about a live-in. Your complex was willing to let you out of your lease given the circumstances, so Mitch and I arranged to have your stuff packed up and shipped to Waketon. If you want to find a place there once you can live on your own, we'll help you get set up. But until then, we think you should stay at the ranch."

"You packed up my stuff? Without asking?" Nicole attempted to stand up but groaned as her body protested. "Please, guys...just...go."

"Nicole..." Carly objected.

"I mean it, Carly. My whole body is one big pile of pain right now and I'm liable to say something we will all regret. I came back to Texas. I wasn't ready to face Waketon yet, and all the people there that still remember. And now I'm being told I don't have a choice!" Nicole closed her eyes as her voice broke. "Please, I need to be alone." She pushed herself back onto the bed and turned her head away from them.

Jack motioned to the others and led the way out of the room. "Did Jason leave?" he asked as they walked outside.

"Yes. He thought it would go smoother if he wasn't around. He said he needed to head back home."

"Not sure it could have gone much worse," Mitch muttered, glancing over his shoulder. "Are you sure we're doing the right thing?"

"No," Jack admitted, with a shrug, "But what are we supposed to do? We didn't lie to her back there. She can't live alone right now and she can't have a live-in where she's at. This is her best option."

"And Jason's?" Carly offered with a smile.

Mitch grinned at his wife as Jack nodded. "And Jason's...if he doesn't screw it up again."

"God help us all if he does," Mitch offered up as a prayer as he led the way to the parking garage, earning an elbow to his ribs from his wife and a chuckle from Jack.

BACK IN HER ROOM, Nicole dried her tears and stared at the blank television screen. How could they think she would be able to just move back to Waketon? She hadn't set foot in that town since graduating from law school. Her childhood had not been a happy one and that had just gotten worse with the deaths of her parents. After that, she couldn't walk through town without people pointing and whispering behind her back. She'd pushed herself to graduate high school a year ahead of schedule just so she could get the hell out of there.

She started to turn onto her side, but the pain in her hips and pelvis stopped her. Groaning in frustration, she pounded the mattress with her fists. "Damn it!"

"Well, now, that doesn't sound like a happy camper." Jack said from the doorway to her room.

She jerked in surprise and frowned at him, "What are you doing here? I thought I told you to go away."

"You did, but I didn't think you meant it." Jack stepped into the room and sat down in the chair by her bed. "Emotional outbursts aren't your style, Nicole. I'm worried about you."

Nicole turned her head so she could see the man sitting next to her. "So you and Mitch just swoop in and start making all the decisions about me *for me*? That's not *your* style, Jack," she held up a hand to stop him before he could speak. "Not even when Mom and Dad died, did I feel like I did today, and I was only 16 then, barely old enough to know *how* to make a decision, let alone be trusted with making any. Yet, Aunt Helen and Uncle Steve always asked what I wanted to do; they made suggestions and they gave advice but they never just moved forward on me without asking me first."

"I'm sorry, Nicole. Really, I am," Jack leaned forward and took her hand in his. "Mitch and Carly and I were just trying to help, honey. You can't live here right now, not by yourself. It just made sense to us to bring you back to Waketon, where we could all help you." He squeezed her hand until she looked over at him. "Just please remember, out of everyone in this patchwork family of ours, I'm pretty much the only one who is going to know how you feel right now about every-single-thing you are going through. I'm an outsider in this family, too; I had to come back to Waketon before I wanted to, lucky to be alive. I had to swallow my pride and accept help from everyone else. And I've had to face my ghosts from the past. Just like you're going to have to do when you go back."

"I know," she whispered, her fingers tightening on his. "I know you guys were...*are* just trying to help me. But my situation is a little different than yours...I'm not a soldier returning from war and being medically discharged, with nowhere else to turn." She pointed out. "And you weren't opposed to returning to Waketon. You don't have the reasons I do to stay away." Letting go of his hand, she brought her hand up to her face, rubbed at her temples. "Sometimes I think it would have been better if my mother would just have sucked it up and not tried to leave. Maybe then dad would at least still be alive."

"No, you'd just have other issues," Jack commented. "Look, your doctors told us there is no way you would be able to drive a car for at least two-to-three months, let alone sit at a desk and work, or stand in court all day. We just thought that we would take some of the stress away, so you could concentrate on healing and recovering. This way, you don't have to worry about covering expenses. All of your short-term disability and insurance money will go to your medical bills—if there are any—and to your savings. We aren't trying to take away your independence."

"What if nothing has changed in Waketon and I can't stay there?"

"It's been over fifteen years, Nicole. But yes, once you

are cleared to drive and live on your own by your doctors, I'll help you move back up here myself." Jack promised her.

"Even if Mitch and Carly don't agree?"

"Even if the rest of the family is against it. But, Nicole, you need to give yourself time to heal and I don't just mean your body. I mean all of you. You've never dealt with all of the issues from your past. Coming back to Waketon now would give you the time to deal with some of those old ghosts and lay them to rest," Jack told her as he stood up. "Look, I can tell by your eyes that you need your next dose of pain meds and some sleep, so I am going to head back to the hotel, for real this time. Are we good?"

"Yeah, we're good." She managed to give him a smile as he leaned down to give her a soft kiss on the forehead. She adjusted the head of the bed and hit the buttons on the side rail to dim the lights, just now realizing how exhausted the last few hours had made her. Maybe Jack was right; maybe going back to Waketon would allow her to lay all of her old ghosts to rest and get over some of those issues that had plagued her since childhood. And she needed to rest so she could deal with those issues and her family that was determined to help her. She hit the button to ask the nurse for her dose of pain medication and said a silent prayer that somehow things would work out.

JACK LEFT the hospital and sat in his silent pickup truck, watching the traffic as it sped by. There was a reason he'd elected not to practice law in a big city and traffic had been at the top of the list. The constant backstabbing he'd seen as everyone tried to get ahead in the private practices hadn't made him a fan of working in the city, either. There was also the added benefit of being his own boss and getting to pick and choose his clients. Small town law was where he belonged.

He hit the button on his phone, allowing it to dial the number he'd pulled up.

"Did you talk to her?" Jason's voice demanded to know as soon as he answered.

"And hello to you, too." Jack spat out a wry rebuttal.

"Sorry. Hello. How's life? Mine sucks. Now, did you talk to Nicole?" Jason repeated.

"God, Jason, are we still in junior high? Should I try and pass her a note between classes next?" Jack was kind of enjoying torturing his friend. He'd never seen him this uptight about a woman before. The fact that it was Nicole, well, he wasn't sure how he felt about *that* quite yet. After all, they had been raised as close as any other siblings, and they knew more secrets about each other than most best friends.

"Jack! Are you listening?" His friend's impatient voice yelled in his ear.

"Yeah, sorry...zoned out for a minute." Jack smothered a yawn. "Yes, Jason, I talked to Nicole. She's upset that decisions are being made about her life without any input from her, but for now she's agreed to come back to Waketon." He heard a rush of breath that was released and almost chuckled. "You need to start setting up the rehab for her and whatever else she'll need. I plan to stick around here for another day-or-so, and then I'll head home. That way I can get the ranch ready for her, have Maria set things up there."

"And then maybe I can figure out what the hell

happened ten years ago and why she kicked me to the curb." There was a resigned sigh over the line. "Dude, I start call tomorrow, so if anything comes up, text me. The way my luck has been running, every orthopedic emergency in ninety-seven counties will happen in the next seventy-two hours.

Jack chuckled and hung up the phone, shaking his head over the knots Nicole still had that poor guy in.

CHAPTER 3

"So, today's the day. Are you ready?" DOCTOR Fredricks asked Nicole as he stepped into her room.

"God, yes!" Nicole was sitting on the edge of her bed, waiting for her family to get there. It had been a little over a month since her accident, and the eagerness to be free of that room had her coiled like a spring.

"With an attitude like that, you're going to make me think you haven't liked your stay here," he told her with a grin.

"I just don't want to overstay my welcome," she returned, as he moved over beside her. He did his last examination and then stepped away from her. "So, do you feel ready? Being in charge of your own rehab is going to be a lot different than having us being right here to make sure you're doing it. And there's a fine line between pushing yourself and going too far," he warned her.

"I know. I'm ready." She nodded. "I remember when Jack was in rehab...I'll be careful."

"I gave the nurses orders to give you a dose of your pain killer right before you leave. That should allow you to sleep through most of your drive. You said it was about two hours, right?"

"Yes. Mitch wanted to fly, but with the way my luck has been running, I was afraid we'd wind up with a delayed flight or stuck on a runway or something. I figured two hours, give-or-take, in a car, was better than the unknown delays that can happen with flying."

"Makes sense. I was supposed to fly from here to Omaha once for a conference. My connection was in Houston, but there were a bunch of summer storms, so I got redirected to Denver and got stuck there for close to six hours. I think I missed the first half of my conference, too." He made a few notations on her clipboard and then set it down on the bedside table. "So, your cousin and friend, Jack, have been pretty scarce the last couple of weeks. Is everything okay?"

"Yes." She looked up at her doctor, confused by the question. "Why do you ask?"

"I just want to make sure you still have the support you need, both physically and emotionally," he explained.

She nodded, pausing before answering. "We're family, we're going to have fights and not speak to each other at times. But Jack, Mitch, and I—and Carly for that matter—would fight the fires of hell for each other. Jack and I have been best friends since my aunt and uncle took him in and became his guardians, back when we were all still toddlers. I'm closer to him than to anyone, even Carly." She shrugged her shoulders, "They'll be there for me."

"Good. Because you're going to need the support. Lean

on them," he advised, offering her his hand. "Come back and see me sometime. I like to see my success stories," he told her with a grin.

"I'll make sure I do that." Nicole smiled back as Carly and Mitch entered the room. The nurses all came in to tell her good bye and wish her luck while Mitch made a quick trip down to the car with all of her stuff. Carly had packed up most of it and taken it back to the ranch earlier in the week so Nicole would have as much room as she'd need to stretch out in the back of the SUV.

Her nurse came in with the promised dose of narcotics and the discharge paperwork before they headed outside. Mitch had dropped one of the seats down so that Nicole could also recline, and they padded the seat with as many pillows as they could and still get a seat belt around her.

"I feel like the Michelin man," she commented as they got the seat belt buckled and Mitch was satisfied that it would be safe for the drive home.

"You're the one who wouldn't fly." he reminded her.

"You're the one who packed up my apartment," she shot back.

"Don't start." Carly rolled her eyes and climbed into the front passenger seat. Nicole stuck her tongue out at her cousin and Mitch grinned at her, closing the rear door before sliding behind the wheel of the SUV and starting the engine. Within minutes, the narcotics they'd given her had kicked in and she was sound asleep. She didn't wake up until Mitch slowed the car to make the turn onto the mile-long driveway up to the main house.

"How are you feeling?" he asked when he glanced in the rear-view mirror and noticed her eyes were open.

"Groggy," she pushed her hair out of her eyes and looked around; she started to shift to a more comfortable position but felt her muscles stiffen. "So, what's the plan for my recovery? The doctors in Austin said you had everything set up for me."

"The physical therapist is going to meet us at the ranch today to do an assessment and see how you're doing. She'll make sure the walker and the crutches are adjusted for you like they're supposed to be. And the orthopedic surgeon at the hospital here in Waketon is going to oversee everything, so you won't have to make any trips to Austin anytime soon," he pulled up in front of the house. "Welcome home, kiddo."

"You okay?" Carly asked her, looking over her shoulder at her as she started to get out of the car, noticing the pained look on her friend's face.

"I'm stiff," she answered, groaning as her muscles protested against her movements as she tried to push herself up. "I'm not sure I can move."

"That's what I'm here for. Carly, please go and open the door for us." Mitch stepped over to the car and gently eased her into his arms. "Relax, easy does it," he murmured when her breath hissed out between her clenched teeth. "We had Maria get the downstairs guest room ready for you, so just hang on. We'll have you inside in no time." Moving up the steps to the front porch as slowly as possible to avoid jostling her too much, Mitch made his way into the house. Carly had gone ahead and turned down the bed and had positioned the pillows so Nicole could sit up.

"Here are some more pain killers, and your muscle relaxer," Carly handed the pills and a glass of water to

Nicole as soon as she was settled. "Maria is making you some soup."

"No more pain killers. They make me too groggy. If the physical therapist is coming, I want to be able to do the exercises," Nicole pushed the pills away. "I'll just take the muscle relaxers for now.

Carly stepped back away from the bed as Maria brought a lunch tray in with a bowl of soup. "Are you sure? Doctor Fredricks said you needed to stay on top of the pain."

"I'm sure. I'll take them later." Nicole promised.

"You going to be okay here? I need to go check in with the boys," Mitch looked between his wife and cousin. Nicole nodded and Carly walked out of the room with him, telling Nicole she'd be right back.

"Is everything ok?" Nicole asked when Carly stepped back into the room.

"Yes. There was a small thunderstorm the other night and the wind took down a few trees and a section of the fence. You know how it is, Steve's away, we've been away, so now he feels like he has to go back and second-guess all the decisions that were made," Carly shrugged.

"So who's my physical therapist?" Nicole asked as she forced herself to eat a few spoonfuls of the soup. She'd found out the hard way in the hospital that taking the muscle relaxers on an empty stomach was not a good idea, but she didn't have much of an appetite since the accident.

"Amy Reece. Remember her? She was a year or so ahead of us in school. We have her on retainer for the hands if they get hurt, so she was willing to work you in today. She should be here soon." Carly said as she looked

23

over at the clock. "I'm going to let you finish your lunch in peace. I'll bring Amy back when she gets here."

Nicole moved the tray away, being careful not to tip the remainder of the soup. With guarded movements, she positioned herself so she was sitting on the edge of the bed. She pushed herself to her feet, keeping a hand on the mattress for balance. Hobbling to the bathroom was a slow and painful process. It wasn't that far, but the muscle relaxers hadn't kicked in and she was still stiff. But some things just couldn't wait.

She took a few minutes in the bathroom to wash her face and combed her hair. She grimaced at the fading bruises that still covered her forehead and cheek where she'd hit the window when her car had rolled. Vanity forced her to try to comb her short bangs over the bruises on her forehead. At least she'd only suffered bruising to her face. She had one laceration on her leg and one on her stomach that had required stitches, and a few other cuts that she thought would leave some scars. But those could be hidden from view with the right clothes.

Feeling more normal than she had in over a month, she left the bathroom and started to make her way back to the bed. She'd made it back to the foot of the bed before her legs started to give out. She was able to grab onto the edge of the mattress and catch herself before she fell to the floor, and managed to sink onto the edge of the bed instead, breathing hard from the exertion of walking a few feet, cursing her own weakness. She waited a few minutes and then pushed herself into a more comfortable position trying to relax and regroup, waiting for Amy to arrive.

Amy did a brief session with her, more to analyze her

strength and see where she was at physically, and promised to return in two days to start their sessions. She told Amy about the near miss while she was there, expressing her frustrations at her limitations, and Amy assured her that the weakness was normal, given her injuries.

"You have to remember, Nicole, you've pretty much been stuck in a bed for...what, almost a month? I bet they let you out of that hospital bed once, maybe twice a day, and only let you walk far enough to get to the bathroom and back to bed, maybe a lap around the hallway if you were lucky. That's not enough to regain any strength. Their goal there was to get you ready to start your therapy with me; they didn't want you to lose any more strength. That's why I'm here," Amy pointed out as she fitted a pair of crutches under Nicole's arms and showed her how to use them. "Now, these are just for use here in the bedroom for now. You need to use the walker 99-percent of the time. Your ribs aren't going to be up to the strain of using the crutches." She pulled it over in front of Nicole and helped her stand up so that she could adjust it and helped her get used to it. She offered to get her a wheelchair, too, if she wanted one, but Nicole refused. Amy made sure she didn't have any questions about the exercises they'd gone over and then gave Nicole her cell number to have on hand, in case anything came up between sessions. With a wave of her hand, Amy headed out the door, and Nicole released a ragged sigh.

NICOLE RESTED for a while after Amy left, the trip to the ranch and the mini-work out having taken their toll.

Unable to stand the pain any longer, she took a dose of the pain medication and woke up a few hours later, feeling a little more refreshed. She glanced at the crutches, but knew her ribs wouldn't be able to handle that kind of pressure. Grudgingly, she pulled the walker over to the bedside and pulled herself upright. She made her way out of her bedroom and down the hall, finding Mitch in his study, alone.

"You're looking a little better than the last time I saw you," Mitch said when he looked up and saw her standing in his doorway. "Come in before you fall in." He stood up and walked around his desk to help her to one of the leather arm chairs. "Did Amy say you could be up like this?"

"She didn't say I *couldn't*. She just said to rest as much as I can. I am not staying in bed all the time," she returned. "I'd like to see you bedridden for a month," she muttered, lowering herself into the chair.

"Now now, be nice to your favorite cousin. I just don't want you to overdo it. Jack told me how bad it was even if you won't admit it. They couldn't tell if there was any nerve damage to your spine until the swelling went down. They kept you in a drug induced coma for four days just to keep you from moving and aggravating that spinal injury. You're lucky to be alive." Mitch sat down beside her, his arm around her shoulders.

"So everyone keeps telling me." She leaned her head back, her eyes closed.

"What's that supposed to mean?" Mitch nudged her.

"Nothing. Ignore me." She could feel Mitch's eyes on her, but she refused to open her own.

"Alright, fine. I'll drop it for now, but I'm not letting

you wallow in self-pity for long. You keep it up, and I'll go find a switch," he warned her, standing up. "Need something to drink?"

"A shot of whiskey would work wonders," she announced, opening her eyes and looking at him.

Mitch shook his head. "You and Jack with that damn whiskey; I'm not giving you alcohol. Not with all the medications you're taking. How about some iced tea instead?" he suggested, heading for the door. He returned a few minutes later with two glasses, handing one to her. He moved over to his desk and leaned against it, studying her. "Your boss told me you called him the day of the accident and gave him your notice," he said after a minute. "I thought you loved your job."

"I do, or, at least, I did. But lately I'd felt—I don't know —restless, I guess," she stared at the ice cubes in her glass. "I traveled three out of four weeks a month, I come back to an empty apartment, and I have no social life to speak of, no friends. I don't ever get to see you and Carly anymore, at least not as much as I'd like to. I decided I wanted to take some time for myself and rediscover *me* again. Not this corporate career woman I've become," she drained the glass. "My boss didn't want to grant an extended leave of absence, so I quit."

"What were you planning to do?"

"I hadn't gotten that far. I had just started packing up my office and left, figuring I'd go back the next day to finish everything, and on my way home I had the accident. So, instead of me packing up my office, I guess someone else did that for me, too."

Mitch cleared his throat and looked out his windows at

the wide open land beyond them. "Yes, your boss was kind enough to have everything sent over to your apartment and I moved it all down here. It's out in one of the empty garage bays," he told her.

"I see." Nicole rolled the glass between her palms, deciding not to pursue that discussion, at least not yet. "So where are Carly and Jack?"

"Carly had to go over to her mother's for a little while. I promised her I'd keep my eye on you. Jack had a client he had to see today. He was able to put off a few meetings while he was up in Austin but now he has to catch up on those meetings and the rest of his work." Mitch stretched his legs out in front of him. "I've talked to your doctor; he wants to see you in his office on Monday morning, just so he can have a baseline to go by. The hospital was nice enough to send all of your records to him, but he'd still like to see you for himself."

"Who is my doctor, anyway? I never thought to ask who was still practicing around here."

Mitch glanced away unwilling to meet her eyes as he said, "Jason."

"Jason? Jason Morrow?" She froze.

"Yeah, my old buddy from Austin that you've managed to avoid for the last decade. That's him. He finished his residency and fellowship in orthopedics and signed on at Waketon Memorial. He keeps himself pretty busy." Mitch glanced over and caught her eye. "Is there going to be a problem?"

She shook her head, lowering her gaze. "No, why would you ask that?"

"Because Jack had to threaten to tie him up to keep him

from storming up to Austin and taking over your care up there, from what I understand," Mitch told her, moving over to stand in front of her. When she didn't look up, he knelt down and forced her eyes up to his. "Look, Nicole, I know you've never opened up to Carly about what went down between you two, and Jason never talked to me about it, but I'm here for you if you need me to listen. And I won't pick sides," he promised, standing up and picking up his Stetson. "I need to go check on some things down at the barn. You going to be okay by yourself for a few minutes? Can I get you anything before I leave?"

She shook her head.

"Okay, well, Maria's in the kitchen, just holler at her if you need anything." With a last glance at his cousin, he settled his hat on his head and headed out of the room, leaving her in a stunned silence.

Jason Morrow. How on earth was she going to face him again after all these years? She leaned her head back and closed her eyes, groaning in frustration. The last time she'd seen him, he'd been pretty upset with her. Okay, to be honest, he had been *pissed* with her. And he'd had every right to be so. She'd broken up with him a few months before her graduation from law school, refusing to tell him why. She'd just stopped taking his calls and refused to see him if he stopped by the apartment. And then when she returned for Mitch's and Carly's wedding, she had avoided being alone with him for much of the festivities even though he was one of the groomsmen and she was the maid of honor. It wasn't until the end of the night, right after Mitch and Carly had made their grand exit that he'd had been able to corner her. She didn't have to try very hard to remember the angry set of his jaw, the glare in his eyes, with maybe a touch of disappointment.

"So that's all I get, a one-sided phone call where you announce that it's over between us? Was this some sort of test that I've failed?" The tone of his voice carried his bewilderment and anger, still there after almost three months.

"No, it wasn't a test. I'm sorry, Jason." She couldn't look into his eyes. "I want a career and a life of my own. You do matter to me, it's just...I mean, I want..." She tried to repeat the reasons she'd been giving herself for the past several months, but her voice had trailed off as he pushed himself away from the wall he was leaning on, towering over her, his hands clenched into fists at his side.

"So, that's it? You're tossing me aside like yesterday's garbage? Well, I hope you find whatever you're looking for in California. But let me tell you this much, sweetheart: when you come to your senses, don't expect me to be waiting around for you. The women are lined up around here waiting for me." He had spat the words at her before storming off.

She hadn't seen or heard from him since. Jack had tried a few times to get her to talk about the break up, usually whenever she was talking about breaking up with whatever guy she was "kind-of" dating at the time, but she'd refused to talk to him about it—probably the only time in her life she'd ever refused to talk to him about something. She was pretty confident that Jack had been a shrink in a previous life.

And now Jason was going to be her doctor? What did Mitch mean when he said that Jack had threatened to tie

Jason up to keep him from coming up to Austin? He couldn't still have feelings for her, could he? If he did have feelings for her, what were her feelings for him? Speaking of Jack and Jason, since when did they even know each other well enough for Jack to threaten to tie the other man up? Hell, this was giving her a headache. She shook her head in frustration. What did she ever do to deserve these complications in her life? Although, that would explain all the times Jack tried to talk to her about her ex, if he was now friends with Jason. With another groan, she pushed herself up and grabbed onto the walker. Maybe if she started walking now, she could get out to the driveway before anyone missed her and then get one of the ranch hands to drive her...somewhere. Her thoughts of escape were interrupted when she heard a car door slam in the driveway and Carly call out to someone.

Damn, she thought to herself, settling back into the couch. *Foiled again.* She looked up at the doorway with a smile as her best friend walked in, determined to once again hide her pain and fear from them all.

CHAPTER 4

Nicole sat on the exam table, nervously waiting for Doctor Jason Morrow to come into the room. She'd already been sitting in the exam room for over twenty minutes by herself. She'd already read every poster on the wall. Twice. It was not helping her anxiety any.

"I'm making too much out of this." She muttered to herself as she realized she was trying to check her reflection in a small mirror over the sink. She'd been trying to get Mitch's comment about Jason out of her mind ever since he'd said it the other day, but it just kept repeating itself. Like a broken record, over and over, she heard Mitch say that Jason had wanted to come to Austin to take over her care. She'd just about managed to convince herself that he was just worried about her because she was Mitch's cousin and Jack's friend. She took a deep breath and held it for five seconds before forcing it out and then turned away from the mirror, as the door to the exam room was pushed open.

"Well well. Nicole Winters. You've started wrestling

with cars now, I see," Jason joked as he walked into the exam room with a nurse.

"Needed something to try and keep in shape-after sitting behind a desk all day," she retorted, her eyes drinking in the sight of him. "Let's just say I learned my lesson. From now on, I'm driving tanks wherever I go." She swallowed around the lump that was all of a sudden filling her throat. "It's been a long time."

"Ten years." He agreed, stepping over to the small sink and washing his hands.

Nicole used the opportunity to study his profile. He hadn't changed much, she realized. Jet black hair, still kept neat and short, although a little longer in the back than it used to be. But he still kept himself in shape, that hadn't changed at all. No dress shirt in the world could hide those muscles. She wondered if he still used the same cologne. How many nights had they cuddled on the couch, with her head on his chest, his arms tight around her, and her just breathing in his scent? Aware of her accelerating heart rate, she swallowed hard and dropped her gaze to the floor, willing her body back under control.

He turned around from the sink and moved over to stand beside her. "I've reviewed the records they sent me from Austin," he said, as he pulled his stool over to the exam table and sat down, while she silently said a short prayer of thanks. At least now she didn't feel as if she were at a disadvantage. She'd almost forgotten how tall he was. At almost six-and-a-half feet tall, he was seven inches taller than her. "This is my nurse, Jodie. She'll stay in the room while I do the physical exam," he explained.

He did a head-to-toe exam, paying close attention to

her ribs. "You took a pretty big hit from the air bag. I want you to continue to use the walker instead of crutches for now. Definitely no driving. Even though nothing was broken in your back it was pretty bruised and you still need to take it easy," he pressed on a tender spot on her ribs, causing her to grimace. "Sorry. Those are the ribs that you broke. Make sure you keep doing those deep breathing exercises they gave you, as well. You're still in danger of developing a pneumonia, if you're not careful." He helped her sit back up and studied her pale features for a split second before turning away from her. He nodded as Jodie indicated she was going to step out. "How are the pain medications working out?"

"Okay, but they make me incredibly groggy, and I feel as if I have a hangover. I don't like to take them. And I've been having nightmares." She gripped the edge of the exam table. She hadn't admitted that to anyone else, although she was sure her screams had woken up Mitch and Carly more than once. "I take the muscle relaxers as scheduled, though."

"Just remember to stay on top of the pain. If you wait too long, the pain killers won't help and you'll be playing a game of catch up. You can cut the dosage of your pain killer in half if you need to. I'll give you a prescription for something else, but it won't work as well." He made some notations in the computer, wrote out a prescription, and then looked up, catching her gaze on him. "How bad are the nightmares? We can make a referral if you need someone to help you through them." He handed the prescription over to her as he spoke.

"They're bad enough to make me not want to take the

pain killers." She started to shrug her shoulders, gasping a little as the movement pulled at her ribs.

"Careful," he cautioned. Her eyes flew to his, the concern she heard in his voice startling her. "I think you should talk to someone. Trauma like you've been through leaves a lot of marks, and not just the visible ones. Talking about it could help you get through it."

"I was talking to a doctor in the hospital and he gave me some names if I need them, but I'm dealing with it just fine on my own."

"Yeah, I remember that about you, you like to do things on your own," the concern she'd heard in his voice was gone now, replaced by cold indifference. "Call the front desk if you change your mind. Therapy isn't always a bad thing, you know," he closed out her chart on the computer and tapped his fingers against the keyboard for a second and waited for her to look up at him. "Do you have any questions?"

"I don't think so," Nicole shook her head. "I appreciate you agreeing to be my doctor." *Even if you do hate me,* she couldn't help but tag on to herself.

"Mitch is still one of my best friends." He shrugged, as if that said it all. "Call if you have any problems or questions," he repeated as he stood up. "I'll see you back later next week. You can make the appointment at the desk on your way out," he added as he opened the door and stepped out, leaving Nicole in shocked silence. He must have gone out to the waiting room and told Carly and Mitch that he was done, because a few minutes later Carly knocked on the exam room door and offered to help her get dressed.

"How'd it go?" Carly asked as she helped her friend adjust the walker and stand up.

"He was very...professional," Nicole told her, grimacing as her ribs protested the movements.

"You sound disappointed," Carly told her, studying her friend's face. "Did you expect him to sweep you off your feet or something?"

"No, but he was almost, I don't know, cold or something. You know, like we'd never met before."

"Well, you haven't seen him in years. You *are* practically strangers again," Carly reminded her.

"I know. And no, I didn't expect him to sweep me off my feet, but I didn't expect cold indifference either," she headed for the door. She stopped at the desk long enough to make the follow up appointment for the following week. Mitch had pulled the car up to the front door and Nicole made her way out to the car.

"Do you need anything while we're in town?" he asked as he pulled out into traffic. "We can get those prescriptions filled."

"No, I don't think so. These are just to replace the others I'm taking, if I want to try them. I'm just ready to go home," she rested her head on the back of the seat.

Mitch and Carly exchanged glances and made small talk the rest of the way home. Once they got back to the ranch, Nicole made excuses about being tired and needing to rest before her therapy session. Carly started to follow her, but Mitch stopped her with a hand on her arm and shook his head.

"Just let her be for a while," he suggested, watching his cousin as she made her way into the house. He wasn't so sure that she would be open to either of them butting in right now, even if it was just to offer a shoulder to lean on. His cousin was almost afraid to show any emotion, afraid it indicated some kind of weakness. And if they pushed her to open up about what she was feeling she might just run away again. Mitch sighed and wrapped his arm around his wife's shoulders, pausing to press a kiss to her forehead. "She'll be okay. We just need to give her time," he promised her.

She nodded before looking up at him with a small smile. "I know. I'll leave her be. For now." She stepped away and headed into the house, leaving him to make his way over to the barn.

JACK WAS SITTING at the desk in his home office when he heard the vehicle pull up in front of his house. The office windows faced the driveway, so he glanced out and watched Jason get out of the pick-up truck and start towards the house. With a muttered curse, he tossed his pen on the desk and moved towards the kitchen door to intercept his friend.

"What are you doing here?" he asked as Jason started to climb the steps to the back door.

"Christ, you scared the crap out of me!" Jason returned, pausing. "Have you talked to her today?"

"No, was I supposed to?" Jack returned, turning away from the door, leading the way into his kitchen. "Mitch and Carly are taking good care of her, I'm sure."

"Have you talked to *them*?"

"No, not today. But didn't Nicole have an appointment

with you today? Did she not show up?" Jack paused and glanced back over his shoulder, a slight frown on his face. He'd go over and read her the riot act himself if she was going to screw around with her health.

"No. I mean, she was at the appointment, but we didn't talk about anything except her medical status. I thought, with as close as you two are, she might have called you." He glanced at his friend.

"Jesus, Jason, grow a pair, would you? You are really starting to irritate the crap out of me," Jack pulled his bottle of Jack Daniels down and added it to the glass of Coke he had in front of him. He tilted the bottle towards Jason, who nodded. Sighing, Jack pulled out another glass, added ice cubes and handed it, the bottle of Jack, and a Coke over to his friend. "I didn't think you drank Jack."

"Most of the time, I don't, but you don't tend to keep scotch around," he reminded him, pouring himself a healthy shot of the whiskey. "I screwed up, my friend."

"Are you just now figuring that out?" Jack raised his eyebrows as he watched his friend swallow the shot in one gulp. "You were the one who let her walk away the last time." Jack pointed out, watching his friend pour another shot. "If you remember, I told you to go after her. Many times."

"I know, and I know I'm to blame for my own misery. You and Mitch have reminded me of that often enough," he drained the glass a second time, grabbed the bottle of whiskey and refilled his glass, before adding a splash of Coke, almost as an afterthought. "And I didn't just let her walk away. She bolted out the fucking door," he muttered, throwing back the third shot. "I mean I screwed up *today*," he clarified.

"How'd you manage that during a...what, fifteen minute office visit? Unless...I don't need to defend anyone's honor here, do I?" Jack glanced over at his friend, the steel in his gaze making Jason take a hasty step back.

"Jesus, no, Jack...fuck, this is so fucking complicated." He knocked back another shot.

Jack shook his head as he watched his friend drink almost his entire bottle of whiskey shot-by-shot. He listened to him as he poured out his feelings for Nicole, knowing that if his friend remembered any of this in the morning, there would be hell to pay. He'd been down this road more than once with this guy.

"How do you get her to talk to you when she's mad at you like this?" Jason asked out of the blue.

"She's never been mad at me 'like this', dumbass. I was never her boyfriend and let her get away from me," Jack told him, shaking his head. "Look, Jason, you need to just go over to Mitch's and sit down with her and talk to her. Let her tell you about her mother. My guess is whatever happened is rooted in her fear of being like her. And if that doesn't work, get her drunk," Jack offered. "But I'll bet you a bottle of Jack Daniels that the talking is all it takes."

"She won't talk to me. She wants her own life and a career," he muttered, reaching for the bottle again, which Jack took from him and stashed in the cabinet. "That's what she told me. What am I going to do, Jack?"

"Christ. You're going to get your ass into bed and sleep this off. And I swear to God, Jason, if you puke in that bed,

I'll shoot you." Jack reached down and hauled his friend to his feet, helping him down the hall to the spare room.

"That's not nice," Jason frowned at his friend, even as he threw his arm around Jack's shoulder. "You're supposed to be nice to me."

"Why, because you're drunk? Get real. You owe me a bottle of whiskey." Jack helped him to the bedroom. "Now go to sleep." He pushed his friend down onto the bed and shook his head. He debated for almost three seconds about calling Nicole and giving her a heads-up but decided against it. He came to the same conclusion that Mitch had earlier in the day: the last time Nicole and Jason had gotten together and things had gotten intense between them, she'd run. If she had time to overthink things, she might pull stakes and run now. And while Jack didn't want Nicole to be hurt in any way, he didn't mind watching this dumbass work a little to get her back, either.

CHAPTER 5

Nicole eased herself down on the porch swing and let out a heavy sigh. Mitch and Carly had left early that morning to attend to some business in San Antonio and weren't planning on returning until sometime the next afternoon. After having to use the walker for the last two months, she had graduated to being allowed to using a cane for support as needed. There were still some issues with muscle spasms in her lower back, but even those were not happening as often as they had been. Now if the damn nightmares would stop so she could get a decent night's sleep.

She looked out over the range, watching with an idle gaze at the cattle and the horses as they grazed. She'd missed this, she realized, looking around; the tranquility of sitting out on a porch, listening to the sounds of the ranch around her. And she missed being a part of it, being a part of the workings of it.

The night before at dinner, Mitch and Jack had asked her to review a couple of contracts for them; she knew Jack was just throwing her a bone. He knew she was ready to go crazy from being inactive for so long. But if he and Mitch were willing to let her review the sale contracts prior to posting and signing them, she was willing to brush up on small town law etiquette. Because she also knew Jack trusted her and wouldn't go back over the contracts. If she said they were good to go, he'd file them for Mitch. So she'd spent most of the morning at Mitch's desk, reading and rereading the simple contracts.

She sighed again and glanced at the watch on her wrist. It was a little after seven o'clock, and she would bet a week's salary—or what used to be her salary—that Jack was sitting at home alone, too, she thought, as she pushed herself up off the swing and walked into the house to find a spare set of keys to the pickup truck Mitch had left parked outside.

Forty minutes later, she pulled the borrowed pickup truck up to the front steps of Jack's farm house. Jack appeared in the doorway as she stepped down from the cab and pushed open his screen door to step out on the porch to meet her.

"Are you allowed to be driving?" he called out to her.

"Nobody was around to stop me." She grinned at him, causing Jack to chuckle.

"You rebel." he watched her as she made her way up the steps. He opened his door for her, tossing his arm around her shoulders as they walked back to his kitchen. "So what brings you all the way out here?"

"Pure boredom. What else?" She headed for the refrigerator and grabbed a beer for herself. "Do you need one while I'm over here?" she asked before she let the door close.

"I've already got one." He indicated the open bottle on the counter top next to him. He picked it up, and studied her across the room. "Boredom, huh? Were you thinking of trying to seduce me, because I have to be honest and tell you as flattering as that is, I'm just not interested."

"No, jackass, I am not here to seduce you," she laughed, shaking her head. Half of this town had had the two of them married off to each other before she'd graduated high school and had been shocked that it had never happened.

"Good. That would just be too weird." Jack took a long pull on his beer, still studying her. "Besides, Jason's my friend, too, and I don't poach."

The statement had her choking on her own beer, and she hurried to set it down on the counter as she wiped the back of her hand across her mouth. "What do you mean by that?"

"Don't try to pull that sweet and innocent act with me. I've helped you get in and out of too many jams to fall for that one." Jack leaned back against the counter and crossed his arms across his chest, waiting. "Don't forget, Nicole, I used to visit you guys in Austin all the time, too. You may have had Mitch fooled about how tight you and Jason were back in the day, but I know better."

"'Back in the day' is right. Jason and I are old news." She told him, wiping off her beer bottle with the kitchen towel she found hanging on the oven handle before taking another drink. "Besides, there's nothing there for you to be 'poaching' on; He pretty much hates me."

"If you say so, but you might want to consider that it takes a lot of emotion to sustain a hate for that long. If it's even hate, which I don't believe it is." Jack shook his head at her. "How are the appointments with Jason going, by the way?"

"Fine. He is the epitome of professionalism. He treats me like he would any other patient," she told him, frowning.

"Any other patient, huh?" Jack studied her across the room. "And that bothers you?"

"No, it doesn't bother me. Why would it bother me? I have moved on. I am one-hundred percent over that infuriating man!"

"Right. That's why you're getting so upset."

"I am not upset!" she told him, her teeth clenched so tight she was afraid they were going to crack.

"Fine, Nicole, you are not upset. But even so, sleeping with you would just be too weird. I mean, you're like family to me. I would wind up needing therapy for life."

"Oh, like you don't already need lifelong therapy, and it has nothing to do with me!" she fired back at him. "I tried to help you out, way back in high school, remember? But, no, you had to date the entire cheerleading squad...in a month! Do you know how many friends you cost me with that stunt?"

"Hey, I was young, and they were willing and we're not talking about me, we're talking about you and Jason," Jack grinned at her.

"There is no 'me and Jason,' either. I told you, he hates me." She drained her beer and slammed the bottle down on the counter. "Got anything besides beer?" She asked, grabbing a whiskey glass out of the cabinet.

44

"Depends...are you looking to get drunk?"

"No. I just want something other than beer if you're going to hassle me about Jason Morrow." She placed a few ice cubes in the glass before looking expectantly at Jack.

He reached up into one of the cabinets and grabbed his bottle of whiskey, handing it over to her.

"Just so we're clear, you drink more than one of those, I get the keys," he told her. She grimaced but dug the keys out of her pocket and set them on the kitchen counter. Jack shook his head, watching her as she poured herself a drink, before turning and leading the way to his living room. "And I am not 'hassling' you. I am just trying to find out why you are so upset over how the good Doctor Morrow is treating you as he would any other patient."

"God, Jack!" Nicole pushed past him into the living room and settled onto the sofa. "I told you, I am not upset! Jason and I ended things a long time ago. We've both moved on. Fate is just being a cruel bitch and threw us back together for a short period of time while I recover. End. Of. Story." She enunciated the last three words with determined precision, narrowing her gaze at Jack before taking a sip of her drink.

"Want to watch a movie?" Jack recognized that look. If he wasn't careful, she would throw something at him or worse, she'd punch him. And when Nicole was mad, she didn't care where or what she hit. He could wind up a soprano. He picked out a comedy from his DVD collection and started the player, settling himself into his recliner.

Jack studied his friend throughout the movie. Something was bothering her, whether it was Jason or being back in this town and having to deal with her old ghosts, he wasn't sure which. He'd picked this movie because it was the kind of comedy she loved. Dry, sarcastic humor and lots of innuendoes to keep you second guessing everything. She hadn't so much as giggled since the opening credits. Opening his mouth to ask her about it, he closed it again. Pressing her about her feelings for Jason was one thing, but he didn't need to rub salt in the wound by forcing her to talk about her parents. He just hoped she'd face these ghosts soon.

By the time the movie ended, Nicole was yawning and Jack refused to let her drive home. Making sure the bed in the guest room was made up for her, they said their good nights. Nicole stretched out on the big bed and tried to get some sleep, but once again the nightmares kept her from sleeping well, and at least once, she woke Jack up with her screams. Sneaking out of the house just as dawn was breaking, she left a note propped up on the kitchen table so he wouldn't worry about her, and headed back to the ranch. At least there she could review those contracts again for Mitch.

THAT AFTERNOON, Nicole was sitting on the front porch when Mitch and Carly arrived home.

"How was your trip?" she called out to them as they climbed out of their car.

"Good," Mitch told her, keeping his arm around his wife's waist as they climbed the steps. "How was your time alone?"

"Fine. I went over to Jack's last night to watch a movie," she raised her eyebrows when they both looked over at the pickup truck and then back to her. "Jason and Amy both gave me the clearance to drive," she reminded them.

"Sorry." Carly at least had the grace to look a little embarrassed. "We just worry about you. We came so close to losing you."

"I know and I appreciate it, but I am fine. I swear." Nicole assured her, standing up to give her a warm hug.

"By the way, Mom called last night; she wanted to remind us that they'll be home on Sunday," Mitch told her, a huge smile on his face as he thought of his parents. "She said Dad's a little nervous about what we've done with the place. I'm thinking of having the boys take down a few fence rails, maybe a hinge off the barn door, just so he feels like he's still needed around the place."

Nicole shook her head as she followed them into the house. "I'm still surprised Aunt Helen was able to convince Uncle Steve to go on this trip, considering your vacation and this humanitarian thing overlapped those first two weeks."

"He knew Jack wouldn't be going anywhere and he trusts him as much as he trusts me. And as hard as he worked convincing Jack that he considered him a second son and all that, he couldn't very well tell Mom that no one was around to keep an eye on things. Not to mention we have an excellent foreman," Mitch pointed out.

"I'm going to go start dinner." Carly gave Mitch a quick kiss and turned towards the kitchen. "What time did you tell Jason to be here?" she asked over her shoulder.

"Around five o'clock. He said not to worry about being fancy!" Mitch called after her, watching Nicole's face drain

47

of color. "What's with you?" he asked, reaching over and touching her arm.

"You invited Jason Morrow to dinner? How could you do that to me?" She turned her wide-eyed gaze on him.

Mitch studied her tightened features for a few seconds before he grabbed her arm and led her into his study shutting the doors. "Sit," he pointed at the chair across from his desk. "Now, spill it," he demanded as soon as she had settled into the seat.

"What?" she asked, picking at a spot on her jeans.

"Don't give me that innocent act. It didn't work when you were fifteen; it ain't going to work now. Explain to me why one of my favorite cousins and my best friend have been acting like idiots all summer. Jason has been my best friend for almost fifteen years. I didn't know I needed your permission to invite him to *my* house for dinner! Besides that, you said everything was fine and there wouldn't be any problems between the two of you. All Carly and I know is that you two went from dating to not speaking to each other in the blink of an eye! Maybe if you were a little more open and honest with us, we would have known not to invite him over while you were in residence!"

"*He* could have said 'no'." She muttered. Mitch leaned back in his chair, raised his eyebrows and stared at her. "Oh, for God's sake, it's been over between us for triple the amount of time that we were even together, but you'd think it all just happened the way he acts. The man hates me, Mitch. Why would he want to come to dinner, knowing I'm here? I don't even know why he agreed to be my doctor, except as a favor to you, Carly, and Jack."

Mitch leaned back in his chair, his eyes narrowing. "What did happen between you two back in college?"

"Not what you're thinking," she glanced away from his all-too-knowing gaze. "He started talking about settling down, having a family." She took a deep breath, looking back at him. "I had just turned twenty-one years old, one of the youngest students in my law class, and nowhere near ready to become a wife and mother. All I could think was, I was going to wind up just like my mother after all, bitter and hating the man I thought I loved. There he was, picking me, the town joke, when it was obvious there were others out there better suited to him: prettier, smarter, sexier," she admitted for the first time, even to herself. "I was scared we were getting in too deep, so I left before it got serious and anyone got hurt."

Mitch nodded and pushed back from his desk. He knew his cousin better than she knew herself at times, and maybe even better than his wife did, although none of them would ever admit it. And he sure as hell didn't know how to deal with her and all these girly emotions she had going on right now. But he could at least give her something to think about.

"You want my take on it? You're still scared and running, but you're not a twenty-something year old kid anymore. So let me set you straight on something. You are not, nor have you ever been, the town joke. What your mom did, and what happened after that, well, it left a lot of people in shock. A lot of people are still upset they didn't realize what was going on before it came to a head. But not one of them blames you or holds you responsible in anyway." He grabbed his hat off the corner of the desk and set it on his head. "I'm going to go check with our foreman and see how things have been going, and then I'm going to go clean up." He walked around the desk, pausing beside her chair until she tipped her head back to look at him. "Nicole, you didn't see Jason after you left, but I did. It *was* serious for him."

She closed her eyes as Mitch stepped around her and left the room. She debated for a moment calling Jack and seeing if she could hang out at his place again, for maybe the next few months until she could get her life straightened out, but that was only delaying the inevitable. Jack's comments to her the night before kept playing through her mind, and she realized that Mitch was right. She was still scared of the feelings Jason had stirred to life in her and she was still trying to run from him and those feelings. And she was tired of running from her past. Even if he did hate her, it was time to put the past where it belonged. Pushing herself to her feet, she headed for her room.

CHAPTER 6

Having spent as much time as possible hiding in her room, Nicole left the sanctuary of her bedroom to join her cousins and Jason in the living room for a drink before dinner. Hearing Jason's deep voice coming from the living room had her stopping in the hallway, out of sight of anyone inside of the room. She wanted to be anywhere else right now.

"I can do this," she whispered even as the fluttering in her stomach increased to epic proportions. She glanced at the front door and wondered how far she could get before Mitch or Carly chased her down. The urge to run was strong. Reminding herself to breathe, she stepped up to the doorway

"Hello, Nicole," Jason greeted her as she entered the room, his eyes following her. "You're moving around better."

"I'm feeling much better, thank you. Almost back to my old self." Nicole agreed, taking a seat on the sofa, next to Carly. "And I've been reviewing some contracts for Mitch to keep my legal skills sharp and to keep me from going out of my mind." She smiled over at her cousin.

"You're at a point where you could go back to Austin and your job, switch to outpatient therapy instead of making Amy drive all the way out here. You just shouldn't travel yet. The time away from your therapy would cause too many setbacks."

He couldn't leave the white coat behind, not even for a night with friends, Nicole shook her head, a rueful grin on her face. "I don't have a job to go back to in Austin," she informed him, raising her eyebrows at him. "I've already resigned my position. Poor Mitch here is stuck with me until I decide what I want to do next. Besides, Amy only makes the drive out here once a week, and she sees some of the ranch hands while she's here. Carly drives me into town for the other two days that I do therapy."

"Wait, you're thinking of not going back to Austin? You didn't tell me that!" Carly exclaimed. "That would be so awesome!"

"We'll see how things go," Nicole answered evaded. She accepted a glass of wine from Mitch with a smile. "Right now, I'm just living in the moment, as the song goes. I will have to find a new job at some point, you know."

Mitch gave her a subtle thumbs-up and then led the conversation away from her by asking Jason a sports question, which led to a heated debate about the upcoming football season. She used the opportunity to observe her ex. He was dressed in jeans and a snug-fitting black polo that showed off the powerful muscles in his arms. For a brief moment, Nicole remembered what it had been like to be wrapped up in them. Maria came to the doorway and announced dinner and the four of them went into the dining room.

Of course, Carly had seated Jason and Nicole across from each other. More than once throughout the meal she felt his eyes on her, and just as often, she found herself looking back at him. What was she going to say to him, if the opportunity arose to be alone with him? There was no way she was going to have *that* conversation with Mitch and Carly hanging around.

"...do you remember that, Nicole?" Carly's voice broke into her thoughts.

"I'm sorry, I was thinking of something else. What did you say?" She jerked her gaze away from Jason, the heat rising in her cheeks as she realized she'd been caught staring.

"I was saying this is just like old times, when I'd come up to Austin to see you and Mitch and the four of us would hang out."

"Except the accommodations are a little classier," Mitch pointed out, waving his hand to indicate the house.

"And roomier. There's nothing like your kitchen also being your living room," he pointed out with a grin.

"And the table doesn't rock. Remember the table you had, Jason, the one that you had to put a folded up piece cardboard under the one leg?" Nicole asked him, smiling across the table at him, feeling her heart jump when he returned it.

"And that god-awful sofa he had, with fabric from the '60's?" Carly laughed.

"Hey, I was living on a budget!" he defended himself. "We all can't be born with a silver spoon in our mouth."

"Umm...except I seem to remember you telling me that you *were*, born with a silver spoon in your mouth, I mean." Carly laughed.

"Well, it wasn't that big of a silver spoon. I still had to live on a budget, and redecorating wasn't in the budget!" he shot back.

"Besides, he was never home. He was always at the hospital," Mitch pointed out, trying to help defend his friend. "He didn't need to worry about his décor."

"Or he was at our place trying to score a meal." Nicole pointed out.

"I never showed up uninvited. Can I help it if Mitch always invited me at mealtimes?"

"When it was my night to cook. You never seemed to show up on his night to cook!" Nicole argued with a laugh.

"Can I help it if you were a better cook than me?" Mitch leaned back in his chair, grinning over at his cousin. "Remember when I caught the microwave on fire?"

"Which time?" Nicole teased, exchanging a look with Carly.

He choked on his drink. "How many times did you catch the microwave on fire?" He asked.

"We went through five microwaves in the four years we shared that apartment." Mitch admitted.

"And now you know why he isn't allowed in our kitchen!" Carly told them, laughing at her husband. "Even Maria knows not to let him in there without supervision!"

She happened to glance across the table at Jason, and their eyes met. For a brief moment, she saw of flicker of interest, or was it desire, in his eyes, but the moment was so brief, she thought she might have imagined it. His jaw moved as if had clenched it and he looked away. Confused, Nicole stared down and pushed the food around her plate. Mitch glanced over at her and saw the bent head and troubled look.

"Well, I don't know about all of you, but I am stuffed." He pushed back his plate. "Anyone else for coffee?"

Jason and Nicole both accepted the offer, and Carly smiled at her husband. "The caffeine isn't...I mean, the caffeine might keep me up. I think I'll stick with water," she told him.

Nicole turned her head towards her friend, shocked. "You're passing up coffee?"

"I haven't been sleeping well since the trip. You know, all the jet lag and stuff, and the doctor told me to cut out the caffeine in the evenings." Carly explained.

Nicole narrowed her gaze.

"So, outside of the office visits with Nicole and at the hospital, I haven't seen you guys since your trip. How was Alaska?" Jason asked as they moved into the living room and Maria brought the coffee in on a serving tray.

"Nice and relaxing," Mitch told him, wrapping his arm around Carly's shoulders and pulling her back against him as he lounged on the sofa. She rested her head on his shoulder and curled her legs up underneath her. They had claimed the bigger of the two sofas, leaving the loveseat and the armchair for Jason and Nicole. "I haven't had a vacation like that in years. I have to admit, I was starting to get a little antsy towards the end, though."

"I'm sorry you had to cut it short because of me," Nicole told them, sitting down on the love seat, surprised when Jason claimed the seat next to her.

"Stop feeling guilty. You would've done the same thing if the situation were reversed." Mitch raised his eyebrow at her in a silent warning, and she remembered his comment from her first day back on the ranch about taking a switch to her. He wiggled his eyebrows at her and she gave him a small smile.

Mitch and Carly described some of the sights they had seen on their cruise, including a pod of whales. After a while, Nicole felt her back start to stiffen, so with a small groan, she shifted and started to push herself to her feet. "I'm sorry, but I need to go take a walk and move around a little. My back is starting to bother me."

"Are you okay?" Jason stood up and extended his hand to her, a silent offer of help. Hesitating for a second, she placed her hand in his and he helped her to her feet.

"I'm fine. I just still get a little stiff if I sit for too long. I've been taking short walks in the evening before bed to help work the kinks out," she answered him.

"Would you like some company?" Jason offered, moving towards the door with her.

Surprised, she nodded and turned for the door. She caught the smug look on Mitch's face as well, but ignored him. They didn't speak for the first few minutes, just walked down to the paddock. The sun was making its descent towards the horizon, and already, the night birds were beginning to stir and the crickets were starting to chirp. He leaned against a post, watching her.

"You look tired. Are you sleeping okay?" he asked, his gaze narrowed as his eyes moved over her. "And you've lost some weight."

"I'm fine. Those pain killers you gave me made the

nightmares worse and they also made me lose my appetite." She shrugged her shoulders. "I quit taking them, and although I'm not sleeping great, the nightmares aren't as bad, and my appetite is starting to come back." She leaned her own weight on the corral post and absently rubbed at her lower back.

"You're far enough out from the accident now you could try Motrin for the pain," Jason suggested. "Are you ready to see someone for the nightmares?"

"No, I'm okay. Honest," she added at his dubious look. "I just keep seeing the crash. It's to be expected, or so I'm told," she lowered her gaze and stared at the ground. He didn't say anything. "At least I'm not waking the entire household up with my screaming anymore." She glanced up at him from under her eyelashes to find him staring at her but his face wasn't revealing any of his thoughts. She sighed and looked away. *This wasn't going anywhere.*

"You woke Jack up last night." He broke his silence and at her surprised look, he shrugged his shoulders. "He's worried about you."

"Is that why you offered to walk with me; because you want to reassure Jack?" She asked, straightening her spine and squaring her shoulders, as if steeling herself against a blow, he thought. It made him stop and think back to the conversation he'd had a few weeks ago with Jack, which despite the amount of whiskey he'd ingested, he'd remembered quite well. He narrowed his gaze and answered her question as much honesty as he could.

"No, I offered to walk with you because I wanted to spend a few minutes alone with you, maybe clear the air and get back onto solid ground, so to speak. The fact that I am your doctor and you are having a few problems just gives us something else to talk about besides our complicated history," he told her, his voice harsher than he intended.

"I'm sorry." She released a ragged breath. "I get a little defensive. I don't want to see any other doctors. The nightmares are starting to get better, and they're not happening every night anymore."

"You'll let me know if you change your mind?" Jason made it a question as he stared at her, trying to read her mind. She gave him a slight nod as she forced her eyes away from his intense stare. They stood there, both leaning against the fence, listening to the sounds of the night.

"Carly's pregnant," she said to fill the silence between them.

"That's my guess, too. That *was* the point of the second honeymoon, I believe," he drawled, a slight grin on his face.

"They've waited a long time," she shifted, her hand again going to her lower back.

"Mitch wanted to wait, since they were married when she was so young, and hadn't gotten to get out of Waketon like you and he did for college. He didn't want her to feel tied down," he agreed.

"I'm guessing he wanted to avoid ending up like my parents," she turned to start walking again and he pushed away from the fence and fell into step beside her.

"Your parents? What about them?" startled, he glanced at her. He hadn't expected her to give him the opening he wanting.

"My parents married when my mom was seventeen, almost as soon as she'd graduated from high school, and she had me less than a year later. She always talked about the things she never got to do, like college or traveling. And of course, Dad was busy working so he never had time to do any of those things with her. They died when I was fifteen," she kicked at a rock on the ground. "Mom always resented Daddy for keeping her from doing what she wanted to do. At least, that's how she saw it. She wasn't a very happy person. I think that's why, when Carly started mentioning wanting to see Alaska and going on that cruise, Mitch encouraged her to plan this second honeymoon. He knows she wouldn't go without him and he didn't want her to feel cheated."

"You never told me about them." Jason led her down a short path to the small creek that ran behind the barns.

Nicole stopped walking, staring out at the shadows. "It was hard talking about them. I was fifteen when they died. I was determined not to wind up like my mother, spending my life looking back and seeing what I hadn't done," Nicole turned and looked at him, deciding in that moment to throw caution to the wind and let him know her thoughts. "I met you and we started hanging out, and then we started dating, and it seemed like before I knew it, you were mentioning settling down and starting a family. Everything my mother had warned me against. I was becoming more independent and all of a sudden, there you were, trying to take control. I saw that independence disappearing, just like my mother had always warned me it would if I ever let a man control my life. I was too immature to try and talk to you, and too scared that you'd be able to talk me into letting you have it all your way, so I left."

He stared at her for a few tense seconds and she began

to wonder if she had imagined seeing that flicker of desire in his eyes at dinner. Maybe it had been annoyance. Or maybe being so honest just now had just pissed him off and she'd ruined everything. "I..."

He reached out and laid a finger over her lips. "Yes, I started talking about settling down and starting a family. I was almost thirty years old. But that didn't mean I was going to hog tie you to the kitchen stove and keep you bare-foot and pregnant!" he reached out and took her hand and pulled her a step closer to him. "I knew you had your own dreams, and I know how hard you worked to get through undergrad and then law school. I mean—Christ, Nicole!— you were twenty-one when you were accepted into law school. I knew how hard you had worked to get there." His hand came up to cup her cheek. "I never asked you to give up your dreams. You just assumed I would and left. You didn't give us a chance."

She stared at him in wonder and then looked away. "I didn't have anything else to go by. And what I felt when I was with you...I was scared," she whispered. "I never even had a boyfriend until you came along."

With a sigh, he tugged on her hands until she stepped into his arms. He wrapped them around her and held her close. "I never meant to scare you away. What I felt for you, I knew it was intense but you were so...secretive, I guess is the word. You never talked to me about your feelings or the past. So much wasted time," he murmured, rubbing her back and shoulders, feeling the tension.

Allowing herself to relax, Nicole leaned into him and he shifted to support most of the weight. He reached up and framed her face with his hands, tilting her head back until he could see her eyes. "We could try again, start over?" he questioned.

Without a word or breaking eye contact, she nodded her agreement.

Jason leaned his head down and rested his forehead against hers. "But this time, we both have to be honest with each other to a fault... and no running away from our problems or our fears. Deal?" he whispered.

"Deal." she whispered back, and he tilted his head and kissed her.

CHAPTER 7

It was like an electric shock the second his lips touched hers. It started slow and tender, and as Nicole began to respond Jason deepened the kiss. After hesitating for a moment, she opened her mouth and met his tongue with her own. His fingers ran through her hair, massaging her scalp. Lost in a sea of emotions, she slid her arms up his broad chest, and then wrapped them around his neck. Pressing herself closer to him as his hands skimmed over her back and down to her hips, she felt the hard ridge of his desire through the layers of clothes. His fingers flexed and bit into her hip pulling her up against him, hard.

He slid one hand up under her shirt, his fingertips skimming along the lacy edge of her bra cup before he placed his whole palm over her breast and started kneading. She gasped, feeling her nipples harden and tilted her head back, allowing him access to the tender areas on her neck. As her hips moved against him, everything else faded away. Nothing mattered but him being here with her.

With a groan, he stopped the sensual assault and held her away from him. "If we keep this up, you're going to be flat on your back on the ground," he explained when she opened her eyes to look up at him in confusion.

"Oh my God." She muttered, stepping back another step. "Jason..."

"It's okay, baby. We have all the time in the world to get to know each other again." He took a step towards her and reached out with a finger and stroked her cheek, then leaned in and gave her a tender kiss. "Okay?"

She nodded, a little embarrassed by her ardent response to him even after all this time. "You always could do that," she muttered, as she ran her fingers through her hair in attempt to restore some order, and not to just to the strands.

"What's that?" Jason reached over and helped tuck a few strands back into place for her.

"Turn yourself off before making that final leap." Nicole was having trouble looking at him and couldn't make herself look him in the eyes.

He stepped in front of her and placed a firm finger under her chin and forced her to look up and meet his searching gaze. "Baby, you were a virgin. It took everything in me not to take you to bed and seduce you. No way in hell did I want you to think you were just a notch on my bedpost. Besides that, you are my best friend's cousin. He trusted me with you," he pulled her back into his arms and pressed his erection against her again. "And for your information, I don't 'turn myself off'. I could lay you down on the ground right now and spend the rest of the night buried deep inside of you, and still be hard as a rock tomorrow morning." Jason studied her flushed face.

With a groan, Nicole buried her face against his chest refusing to look up at him. Chuckling, he wrapped his arms around her. "Now, let's go back up to the house before Mitch feels the need to send out a search party." He turned her around, and, linking his fingers through hers, led her back up to the house. "I don't think I could take any comments from Mitch right now, so I'm going to go ahead and get out of here. I'll call you tomorrow," he whispered against her lips when he leaned in for a goodnight kiss.

"I'd like that." She nodded returning his kiss.

With a soft groan, he took a step back from her, gave her a wink, and then gave her a gentle push towards the door. "Tomorrow," he promised her as he headed back down the steps to his truck.

She watched as his taillights disappeared down the drive before turning to the door, but decided she wasn't quite ready to head inside. Walking over to the porch swing, she sat down. With a push of her foot, she set it into motion and then watched the stars as they started to fill the evening sky. Not even in Austin were the stars this bright or numerous.

It had been a night much like this one when she'd been told her parents were dead. The day had been spent at the lake with some friends, doing the typical teenager-on-summer-break thing. Thinking she was going to catch hell for being late, Nicole had rushed into the house. But to her surprise, the house was empty. She'd called Aunt Helen and Uncle Steve, thinking maybe they had gone over there. But Helen hadn't heard from her sister in days. Helen checked with Uncle Steve and said that her father had left the job around noon that day, claiming he had personal business to attend to.

"Do you want me to come over and wait with you?" Her aunt had asked.

"Oh no. I'm sure they'll be home soon." Nicole had assured her. "I'll have Mom give you a call tomorrow."

She had taken a cool shower before making herself a sandwich. Because her father didn't believe in air conditioning even with the Texas heat, she had taken a large glass of ice tea and a new book out to the front porch and sat on the porch swing. There was always a gentle breeze in the evenings that helped cool things off. She settled into her favorite reading position on the swing and had been reading for a while when she heard the sound of a car coming slowly down the ranch road.

It wasn't her father's pickup truck, she'd realized, so she stood up and moved to the railing. A sense of foreboding swept over her when she saw the distinctive lights on the roof of the car. Her grip tightened around the porch railing as she watched the Sheriff Aunt Helen and Uncle Steve exit the car. She watched as they approached the house. Helen had looked up, and seeing the grief on her face Nicole had known without a word being spoken that something awful had happened to her parents.

"Nicole..." Helen hurried up the steps and put her arms around her niece.

"Tell me." She pushed away from her aunt, her gaze on the sheriff.

"Nicole, I am sorry to be the one to have to tell you this...There was an incident involving your parents." The

Sheriff cleared his throat, looking at her aunt and uncle. "Nicole, your parents...were they having problems, do you know?"

Nicole looked between the three adults. Aunt Helen was twisting her hands together and Uncle Steve looked like he was ready to throw up. *What is going on?* She looked back at the Sheriff. "Well, they always argued about money and mom wanted dad to take more time off. What do you mean by problems?"

Uncle Steve looked at the Sheriff, who nodded curtly at him. "Nicole, your mom was trying to leave today. She called your dad at lunch time and he took the afternoon off, told me he had personal business." Now it was Uncle Steve's turn to clear his throat. "I don't know how else to say this, honey, but your dad followed your mom and it looks like they argued. The police will do more tests but they think he shot your mom and then shot himself."

Her vision had narrowed down to just the sheriff in front of her. She could see everyone's lips moving but the words weren't making sense. A roaring sound filled her ears and her vision blurred before she blacked out. She remembered bits and pieces of the next few days as she moved through them in a haze of grief and shock. Aunt Helen and Uncle Steve had bundled her up and moved her over to their house and had taken care of all the details for the funerals and burials. She hadn't returned to her parents' house since that day. Uncle Steve had gotten a couple of his ranch hands to pack everything up for her. They'd sold off anything of value that she didn't want. The rest was boxed up and still in the attic here at the ranch, waiting for her to go through it all.

. . .

SHE WAS THRUST BACK into the present when her cousin sat down next to her on the swing. Letting out a screech of surprise, she turned her head to glare at her cousin. She'd been so wrapped up in thoughts of the past, she hadn't realized he'd joined her.

"What are you doing, sneaking around in the dark like that?"

"It's my house; I can sneak if I want to. Besides, it isn't dark yet." Mitch settled onto the swing with her. "What are you doing out here by yourself, are you okay? Where'd Jason go?"

"You can stop asking me that all the time. I'm fine." She pulled her legs up and wrapped her arms around her knees. "Jason decided to head on home. I think he was afraid of what you'd say if he came back in with me." She paused and turned her head to meet her cousin's knowing look. "He wants us to start over and to try again."

Mitch studied her for a few brief seconds before speaking. "Nicole, I stayed out of it the first time around, but this time I am going to give you my opinion, whether you want it or not," he paused for a second, looking out at his ranch before turning back to her. "Before you start anything, you need to figure out what *you* want and where Jason fits into that equation. I know you want to be happy and not to have any regrets when you look back at your life. But, honey, that's part of life. We all have regrets. I know what your mother used to say to you about love and marriage, and how it was all a trap. But for some reason your mother was not a happy person and she refused to try to change that. Don't let her continue to dictate your life from the grave," Mitch stretched his arm out across the back of the swing, his foot starting the motion of the swing up again. "If that's here and with Jason, then great. If it's not, then tell me what you need my help with, and you know you've got it."

"Mitch, right now, the only regret I have is staying away from this town for so long and listening to that voice in my head telling me to never trust someone who says they love you," she answered him. "You know what a miserable childhood I had. I realize now that I have been running from it. Being back here, being able to remember some of the good things from my childhood instead of just mom's anger and hatred, well, I'm beginning to let go of the past. I just wish..." She swallowed hard around a sudden lump in her throat. "I just wish Daddy were still here to answer some of my questions, you know? Like how did he ever fall in love with someone like her, or what changed her? And why did he do what he did?"

Mitch curled his fingers around her shoulder and she laid her head on his shoulder and they sat there for a few silent minutes, the soft creaking sounds of the swing blending with the other night sounds.

"Mom might be able to answer some of those questions for you, you know. She's made comments over the years about how much your mom changed, but whenever she realized I was around, she'd stop talking. But I think if you were the one to ask the questions, she'd talk to you."

"I have asked a few questions. Maybe it's time I asked a few more pointed ones," Nicole agreed, thinking about her parents.

"So, what *are* you going to do about Jason?" Mitch asked after a few more seconds of silence had passed.

She stopped the swing and stood up. "I'm going to take it one day at a time and see where life leads me. I can't change what I did before but I hope I've learned a few things since then, about life and myself," she leaned over and kissed her cousin's cheek. "I know you care, and I appreciate it. And thanks for listening."

"Anytime, kiddo." Mitch smiled up at her. "Hey, Carly asked me to tell you to stop in the den on your way inside. I think she wants to 'chat' with you about our friend Jason." He gave the air quotes with a slight smirk. She laughed at him and headed inside to find her friend.

Carly was still in the den, but she had drifted off to sleep with her book on her lap, a finger tucked inside marking her page. Nicole reached down and eased the book out of her friend's grasp. Carly woke up as she was tucking an afghan around her.

"Oh, I didn't mean to fall asleep. Not having caffeine in the evenings is working," Carly mumbled around a yawn. "How was your walk with Jason?"

"Fine." Nicole sat down beside her friend, handing the book back to her, and gave her a knowing smile. "I'll spill if you spill." She offered.

"You've already figured out my secret, haven't you? I saw the look you gave me when I turned down that coffee." Carly pushed her hair back out of her eyes. "I'm thirteen weeks pregnant and everything is going well," Carly admitted. "Now, about you and Jason..." she prompted.

"We took a walk, and had a nice little talk..."

"You were hot and heavy back in college and now you're picking up the pieces," Carly supplied for her.

She stared at her friend in stunned silence for a minute and then started laughing. "I guess that's one way to summarize it.

Carly stretched her arms up above her head. "So, give me the details!"

"There aren't any details yet. We're going to try and take it slow. I need to figure out what I want to do," she told her.

"Try saying that without a blush and swollen lips," Carly teased, and Nicole blushed even more as she raised a hand to her mouth to touch her lips, much to Carly's amusement. "So?

"So, we went for a walk and he kissed me. And we're going to continue talking and see where we go from here." She closed her eyes. "And it scares me to death!"

"Not surprising since you had such a lousy example of love growing up." Carly reached over for her glass of water on the end table.

Nicole nodded. "I know. Mitch just gave me pretty much the same speech outside."

"Smart man, that husband of mine." Carly grinned over at Nicole. "Look, Nicole, neither of us wants to butt in where we are not wanted..." she paused as if collecting her thoughts. "We just want you to be happy, hon. Whether you stay here or move somewhere else and continue your career, Mitch and I will always be there for you," Carly stood up and folded the afghan and placed it over the back of the couch. "I would love to sit up with you and list all of the pros and cons of both options, but being pregnant just sucks every last ounce of energy out of me. I am going to bed. But come tomorrow I am all ears!" Carly gave her shoulder a pat as she passed by, leaving Nicole alone with her thoughts.

Nicole sat in the living room, the only sound the ticking of the clock on the mantle. The front door opened and closed and she heard Mitch's heavy tread on the stairs. So much information had been put out there tonight, she didn't know what to think, or how to start processing it all. Should she take this chance with Jason or continue to protect her heart? God, she was so confused. It was a hell of a lot easier when she just didn't care and put all of her time and energy into her career.

The phone rang a few minutes later, jolting her out of her thoughts and she reached over and answered it. "Williams' residence."

"Hi, baby," Jason's voice rose at the sound of hers. "I was hoping you'd answer so I wouldn't have to put up with Mitch and his jokes."

"You'll have to anyway. I picked up the extension," Mitch's voice sounded over the wire, causing Nicole to gasp and Jason to chuckle. She heard Carly's soft voice in the background telling Mitch to be nice and hang up the phone. "Don't melt my phone with the heavy breathing." Mitch warned making his disconnect audible.

"Sorry about that," Nicole whispered. "I have a feeling he is going to pay me back for all of the torment I caused him when we were younger."

"Why are you whispering?" Jason asked her, still chuckling.

"I don't know." She moved out to the side porch and

looked out at the stars again. "Why did you call? Not that I'm not happy to hear your voice. I mean… " She groaned. "Why do I feel like I'm sixteen again?"

"I just wanted to hear your voice again to make sure I hadn't scared you off," he told her, chuckling.

"I'm not running this time," she promised closing her eyes against the rush of emotions the warmth in his voice caused her.

"I'm glad. We have a lot we need to talk about and the phone is not how I want to do it. How about I take you to dinner tomorrow night? There's a new steakhouse out by the interstate we could try."

"It's a date." She agreed. "Jason…"

He waited a few seconds but she didn't say anything else. "Talk to me, honey. Total honesty, remember?"

"Jason, I'm petrified!" She admitted with a groan. "What if—?"

"'What ifs' are what got us here to begin with, baby," he interrupted her. "All I am asking for is a date for tomorrow night. A little dinner, a little conversation. That's all. Okay?"

She released the breath she'd been holding. "Okay. Are you sure you can put up with me and my hang-ups?"

"I am only asking for the opportunity to give it a shot," he told her with a chuckle. "Listen, babe, I have to be at the hospital early tomorrow for rounds. Take care of yourself and I will see you tomorrow night."

They hung up and she moved back inside and returned the phone to its cradle. She stepped out into the hallway and ran into Mitch.

"You into eavesdropping now? I thought you were upstairs."

"I was. Carly forgot her water." He held up the glass in his hand. "I trust my phone is still operational?" he asked grinning at her obvious embarrassment.

"Yes, he just called to ask me to dinner tomorrow night." She stuck her tongue out. "You promised to be nice."

"I promised to not butt in, I never promised to be nice. That's too much of a stretch!" Mitch tossed.

Laughing, she went into her bedroom and got ready for bed. Climbing under the covers, her thoughts drifted once again to her past. After the murder-suicide of her parents, she'd become withdrawn. She left the ranch to go to school, or when her aunt and uncle insisted. That was it. Four years of high school were completed in three. College had been her chance to get away from Waketon and her past. No one in Austin knew her or what her father had done. She'd wanted it kept that way.

And then Mitch had introduced her to Jason, and she'd started to wonder if maybe, just maybe, her mother had it all wrong.

"Never trust a man. He will steal your identity, make you settle down, start a family when you don't want to. Marriage is a death sentence, Nicole. Don't ever fall into that trap." Those were the lessons her mother drummed into her, the legacy she'd left her.

But Jason had pushed past the walls she had built up. He had never laughed at her inexperience. The few times she had swallowed her fears about sex and allowed things to progress beyond just kissing, he had been gentle and encouraging, not taking any more from her than she'd been willing to give. But she couldn't let down that final wall. Convinced at the time that Jason was not that into her, she'd held back, thinking he was just after getting laid. It had never occurred to her that he may have talked to Mitch and had insight into her upbringing.

But now she did know, she thought to herself, a soft smile on her lips, thinking of their walk. Her stomach still had the butterfly feeling going on from that kiss. Amazing how one simple decision to listen to her heart could change everything.

And now, she and Jason were getting a second chance. With any luck, this time she was going to get that 'happily ever after'- ending all those bedtime stories from childhood promised, she told herself as she snuggled down deeper under her covers. She still had to face the fear she had of disappointing him if they did make it as far as having sex together. God only knew what other hang ups of hers were going to rear back up. She still needed to tell him that although she was no longer a virgin, she might as well be. They'd sworn to be honest with each other. But that was one conversation she was not looking forward to having with him. She was pretty sure she was going to die from embarrassment. On the spot. Immediately. She groaned, pulled a pillow over her head and prayed for sleep. Or suffocation.

CHAPTER 8

Nervous and antsy, nicole checked her reflection in the mirror as Carly reclined on the bed in her room. Nicole smoothed her hand over her stomach again, praying to every god she could think of that she wouldn't throw-up. She was going to be alone with Jason. On a date. Swallowing hard, she met Carly's eyes in the mirror.

"Are you sure...?" Nicole was still self-conscious of the visible scars on her legs, even though she knew the dress covered them. At least for therapy appointments, she could wear her baggy sweatpants to cover everything. "Maybe I should change back into that other one?" Her hand reached for the buttons on the bodice of her dress.

"Don't you dare! You've already changed your mind ten times, and I'm telling you, that dress is perfect!" Carly pushed herself off the bed and came over to stand beside her, reaching up to tuck a stray strand of hair back into place. "Jason is not going to be able to take his eyes off of you, not to mention his hands. Trust me. Have I ever steered you wrong before...about clothes, I mean? Now quit acting like a teen on prom night," she handed Nicole her purse and pushed her towards the bedroom door. "And go out to the living room and wait for your man. He will be here in a few minutes."

Nicole took a deep breath and squared her shoulders, attempting to settle the butterflies that were insisting on taking flight in her stomach.

"Hey, you clean up nice!" Mitch offered up as they entered the living room, joining him and Jack. "So where's Jason taking you?"

"He said something about a new steakhouse." Nicole sat down on the sofa, but within seconds was up and pacing.

"You trying to work up an appetite or something?" Jack chuckled, watching her.

"What?" Nicole turned around and looked at him.

"That endless pacing you're doing," Mitch indicated with a wave of his hand. "Sit down and relax for a few minutes. Do you need a drink?"

"No, thanks."

"I was talking to Jack," Mitch teased handing his other cousin a beer.

"Quit teasing her, boys." Carly swatted at her husband's arm as she moved by him to sit next to her. "Ignore them, Nicole."

"I'm trying. What time is it?" She twisted her head to look at the clock just as she heard Jason's truck pulling up outside. "He's here." Feeling helpless, she looked at her friend as Mitch and Jack started chuckling again. Mitch got to his feet and went to greet Jason.

"Relax, Nicole. It's just a dinner with an old friend." Jack leaned forward, snagging her hand and tugging her around to look at him. "You'll be fine." He gave her a wink as Mitch and Jason stepped into the room.

"Hi, everyone," Jason greeted them but his eyes were already on Nicole. "You look great," he told her, stepping over and giving her a soft kiss.

"Told you." Carly leaned over and whispered for Nicole's ears alone.

"Have time for a drink?" Mitch asked, as he reclaimed his seat and his beer. "Jack and I were just going over some of the stuff we need to tell Dad when he and Mom come home on Sunday."

Jason looked at Nicole, but she shook her head. "No, we should just go ahead and get going," he helped her to her feet and tucked her hand in his and started to lead her out.

"You two have a good time," Carly told them.

"Have her home by midnight," Mitch called after them.

"Before she turns back into a pumpkin!" Jack put in.

Nicole gave him a look that could kill and held up her hand in a one-finger salute. Jason squeezed the hand he was holding and led her outside to his truck and helped her in. "You do look great. Is it ok if I kiss you in front of them?" he asked pausing before he shut the door.

"Who?"

"Your family. I'm sure they're watching out the windows." He leaned over and gave her a soft kiss before moving back and shutting the door with a wink. He went around the front of the truck and opened his door and got in behind the wheel. "How's your back feeling tonight?"

"It's okay. I made sure I did all of my stretching exercises and I took a couple of short walks today to try and keep things loose. As long as I remember to stretch and move around as much as possible during the day, it doesn't bother me that much," she assured him as he started the engine and drove away from the house.

"That's good to know. I know Amy has been pleased with your progress, and based on what I've been seeing, so am I. What else did you do today?" He slowed down as he approached the main road, checking the traffic in both directions.

"Not a whole lot. I was so bored, I offered to look over herd records for Mitch and input them into the computer for him. Now *that's* fascinating information, let me tell you," she replied with enough sarcasm in her tone to get a chuckle out of him. "How was your day?"

"Good. I had to attend morning rounds at the hospital, but it was a relatively slow day, so I was able to get a lot of my paperwork done," he reached over to take her hand, lacing his fingers with hers. "And I spent a lot of time thinking about you."

"Really? All good things, I hope." She looked over at him, and he flashed her one of his devastating grins, the warm look in his eyes causing her to blush. It occurred to her how insincere she'd just sounded. "That's sweet. I've thought about you a lot today, too," she admitted, fighting through the shyness to maintain her smile. "Mitch and Jack were having fun teasing me before you got there, and Carly said I reminded her of a teenager on Prom Night, because of how nervous I was."

"Why are you so nervous? It's just me, remember?" He gave her hand a squeeze as he drove towards town.

"It's *because* it's you," she admitted. "I haven't felt like this in over ten years. One of the reasons my back was bothering me last night was because I was so stressed about seeing you again. I wasn't sure how you were going to treat me. Plus, I had already decided I was going to try and talk to you alone," she tried to explain.

He glanced over at her and smiled. "That is some pretty powerful ammunition you're giving me," he warned her as he steered into the parking lot of the steakhouse. He cut off the engine and turned towards her. "Listen, Cole —" he slipped back into the nickname he had called her before —"I promise we will go as slow as you need to this time. As slow as you need to, but you need to promise me you will be honest and let me know what you are feeling." He reached over and stroked a finger down her cheek. "I let you get away once. I am not sure I can do it again."

"I'm not sure I want to get away this time. I've seen the outside world. It's not for me," she told him, her heart racing at just that tender caress.

Their gazes held for a few seconds before he opened his door, sliding out. He studied her for a few more seconds before he opened his door and slid out. Coming around to her side, he helped her down from the cab and led the way inside. The hostess seated them in a secluded corner, handed over the menus and listed the specials. Using the time Jason's attention was on the hostess, Nicole attempted to get her heart rate back under control.

They made small talk until after they placed their orders and were waiting for the appetizers to arrive. "So, up until yesterday, I thought I knew all about you, but you threw a couple of curve balls at me last night. I want to know more about your childhood." He reached over and took her hand rubbing his thumb over her knuckles.

"It wasn't all sunshine and roses." She felt him give her fingers a squeeze, as if to encourage her. She took a deep breath and continued. "I'm planning to ask Aunt Helen some questions when she and Uncle Steve get back, see if she can help me figure some of this out. I know she and my mom weren't close and I know their dad walked out when Mom was pretty young. Mom didn't talk much about it, though. My own educated guess is that she was jealous of Aunt Helen and Uncle Steve and thought that money would buy happiness," her free hand played with her place setting. "I can't remember a time when they weren't fighting over something. Mom always wanted to go shopping or take lavish vacations. Daddy always said 'No'. The police think she was trying to leave him the night they died," she shook her head and raised her eyes to his. Expecting to see pity, she was surprised to see nothing but compassion. Wondering if the gossips in town had told him yet about her parents and how they died, she broke eye contact. Knowing she needed to tell him and telling him were two different things. She couldn't do it yet.

"After they died, I let Uncle Steve make most of the decisions for me about my ranch, and he invested the money for me. A chunk of my inheritance went towards my education, and the rest of it was invested. I make a good living now, so it's just been sitting there, earning interest for me. It's funny—in a really sad, depressing way— but in their deaths I got the financial freedom she always wanted for herself."

"So, you decided to head for Austin and UT, where you met me, and then you graduated and left the state. Fill me in on what's happened since then," he invited, his thumb still stroking over her knuckles.

"It's pretty boring." She warned him taking a sip of her wine to fortify herself. "I moved to San Diego with the law firm and started learning the ins and outs of big time contract and business law. I traveled extensively all over the country. I would fly from San Diego on Sunday afternoon to New York, back to San Diego on Tuesday, out Wednesday morning to North Carolina, back to California by Friday, and back out somewhere else by Sunday again. That was my life, even after I moved back to Austin. Its why, even before my accident, I had decided it was time to take stock and reevaluate my life. I want to find something else that interests me." She leaned back when the waiter appeared with their appetizers.

"Like what?" He gave her fingers a squeeze before letting go to pick up his fork to start to eat.

"I don't know. There's got to be something out there for me somewhere. To be honest, I haven't thought about it that much. I just don't want to do the endless travel anymore, always living out of suitcases." She shrugged her shoulders and gave him a brief smile. "So, now I'm here and I've got no immediate plans for the future."

"How fortuitous for me." He grinned at her. "That gives me plenty of time to convince you to stay in Waketon."

She smiled back at him. "Now, it's your turn. Tell me about yourself."

"Oh, my story is even more boring than yours. I finished up my residency in Austin, spent some time back in Houston and Galveston, and then got the job here in Waketon. Mitch and I have been best friends since we met and it made sense to move here when the opportunity arose. My only family to speak of is a much younger half-sister who currently lives out of the country, with her loser boyfriend and his band," he explained as he leaned back to allow the server to switch out their appetizers for their dinner plates. "Are we going to gloss over our personal lives?"

"I was going to, yes," she told him, taking another sip of the wine.

"Honesty, remember?" He took a drink of his own wine, tipping his glass towards her.

"That was being honest," she pointed out with a smirk, but at his raised eyebrow, she gave in with a slight laugh. "OK, well then, honestly, I want you to go first this time." She leaned back in her chair as the server placed her dinner in front of her. He waited while they cut into their steaks to check that they were cooked to their satisfaction, refilled Nicole's wine glass, and then faded away.

"I wasn't a monk, Cole," he told her. "The way you left, the way *we* left things, hell, I never expected you to return here and I never expected us to give it another try."

"I don't think I would have expected you to be a monk, any more than you expected me to be a nun. Like you said, I left and I hadn't planned on coming back," she agreed, keeping her voice low. "So, you've had girlfriends..." she prompted.

"So, I've had a few girlfriends and one serious relationship in the last ten years." He paused to take a few bites of food.

"How serious?" she asked him feeling a few faint jabs of jealousy.

"She and I lived together for a couple of years. She broke it off when I wouldn't propose to her."

"Why wouldn't you propose? You must have loved her, you were living with her. And I know how much you wanted to get married," she reminded him. She wondered if he could see the jealousy in her eyes. *How can I be jealous? I pushed him away, refused to deal with the issues. I don't have the right to be jealous.* She cast a couple of glances towards him from under her eyelashes as they ate in silence. He seemed lost in thought.

"I realized that I was fond of her, I loved things about her, but I wasn't *in love* with her. She was comfortable to be around, she put up with my schedule, but..." Jason broke the silence. "Anyway, I started talking about moving to a small town, like Waketon, and she didn't want to leave Houston. So we parted ways."

"And that was it?" *If he didn't pick up on the jealousy before now, that tone of voice was sure to clue him in.*

"That was it," he gave her a crooked smile. "She wasn't the one, Cole."

Her heart stopped and then restarted at twice the normal pace. She bit her lower lip and tried to smile back. *What the hell does that mean? Is he thinking I'm the one?*

What the hell do I do with that? She laid her fork down and pushed her plate away as he did the same.

The waiter approached and offered dessert, but they both turned it down. He cleared their plates and brought the check. Jason didn't even glance at it, just handed over his credit card. He started to say something, but then paused.

She reached her hand across the table and touched his arm. "Now it's my turn to remind you to be honest," she told him.

"I wanted to marry *you*, Cole. When it came down to it with Sara—like I said, I realized I was fond of her, comfortable with the way things were. I had no desire to change things," Jason's eyes were full of the same fear, confusion, and hope that had her so tied up in knots.

Her breath hitched at the depth of his emotions. *I've got to tell him. Before this goes too far. I can walk away now, but I won't be able to if we keep going.*

The waiter returned with the charge slip which Jason scrawled his name across before grabbing his copy and standing up.

"Come on." He held his hand out to her and led her out of the restaurant and into the cab of the pickup. He cupped her face with his hand. "Come home with me?" he asked, holding her gaze.

She lowered her head, away from his searching eyes. She had to tell him the rest of her story. But she couldn't go back to his place if he was thinking something else would be happening. Reaching over, she placed her hand on his chest, his heart beating out its steady rhythm. "I'm not..."

"I'm not asking you to, I just want to spend some time

alone with you. I'm not ready for the night to end, Cole," he laid his hand over hers, trapping it against his heat. Pressing her lips together, she nodded. He brought her hand up to his mouth and kissed her fingertips, stepped back and shut her door, walking around to the driver's side.

"So where do you live?" she asked.

"I bought a condo out by the lake. It's small," he navigated his way through the parking lot and headed for the highway. "But it suits my needs for now. I've thought about buying up some land, building my own house, but haven't found the right spot." He reached over and took her hand, interlacing their fingers together. "I'm giving you fair warning, Nicole. We are going to finish that conversation."

"Which one?" She glanced over at him. *Did he already know?*

"I want to know everything about you, even if you think it is going to hurt me." He entered the condominium complex through the gate and parked in front of his garage. "Home sweet home."

He led her inside and took her into the living room, turning on a single lamp which cast a very soft glow across the room. "Have a seat. I'm just going to get a bottle of wine," he indicated the sofa and headed for the kitchen. She stood in the middle of the room and looked around. The room was very impersonal, similar to her apartment in Austin. She stepped over to the large window that overlooked the lake. Lost in her thoughts she wasn't aware he had returned until he set the wine down on a table and stepped up behind her. He wrapped his arms around her waist from behind her and pulled her back against him, just holding her in his arms, letting her feel his strength.

"I warned you I had hang ups." She sighed, relaxing against him, laying her arms over his.

"Tell me what you need, Cole. I'm not going anywhere." He nuzzled her neck.

"If you want my story, you've got to stop that. I can't concentrate..." Nicole warned, although she tilted her head to give him better access.

He chuckled and dropped his arms. He reached for the wine and the two glasses he had brought out and turned to her. "Come on, sit down and relax." He took her arm and led her over to the sofa, waiting for her to get comfortable before removing the cork from the wine bottle and pouring them each a glass. He handed her a glass and then sat down beside her, wrapping his arm around her shoulders and pulling her against him. "So, now that you don't have to look at me while you answer me, tell me about your personal life."

She took a fortifying sip of the wine. "There is so much about me you don't know. Things no one outside of this town knows about me." Glancing at her wine glass, she leaned forward and set it on the coffee table. As much as she wanted to guzzle it, this was one conversation that needed to be had without the influence of alcohol.

"I mentioned earlier that the police thought my mom was trying to leave my dad the night they died." She paused, collecting her thoughts. He set his own wine glass down and wrapped both arms around her, offering support. "Someone called the police saying they'd heard gunshots coming from an old feeder road that ran behind their property, so Sheriff Parker went out to check it out. My mom's car and my dad's truck were there, mom's had a couple suitcases in it with a bunch of her clothes..." Nicole had to stop and swallow hard before she could continue. "She'd been shot in the chest, up close. And then he turned the gun on himself."

"Your dad—"

"They said he must've found out she was leaving and followed her." She closed her eyes against the memories of what the police had told her. "A crime of passion, that's what they called it. Probably more passion in that moment than had been between them in years." She gave a bitter laugh and allowed her head to fall onto his shoulder. Feeling his arm tighten around her, she drew in a shuddery breath. "She hadn't left a note, not even to say she was leaving us. And he wasn't around to say why..." her voice broke and she struggled to get herself back under control. She was afraid to move her head, to see his reaction. Other than his arm tightening around her, he'd been silent and unmoving.

After a slight hesitation, she continued. "From that point on, I stayed on the ranch as much as possible. I hated going to town and having people look at me and talk about me as if I didn't know what they were thinking. I would have quit going to school if they'd have let me. And dating was out of the question." Her hand was on his chest and her restless fingers smoothed over the fabric of his shirt.

He laid his hand over hers on his chest, stilling her fingers. "So was I your first date?" he smiled at her as he asked.

With a soft laugh, she shook her head. "No, not my first date. Jack, Mitch, and Carly made sure I went out enough to keep from being a hermit. But you were my first boyfriend," she admitted as she laced her fingers with his. "You know what life was like for me in Austin, you were there. I pushed myself to get through undergrad so I could go onto law school, and then after graduation, I took that job in California and headed out there as fast as I could."

Needing to see his face, she sat up and turned her body to face him. "I wanted to forget you, forget everything about Texas. I worked my ass off for that law firm, taking on extra duties if it meant I didn't have to think up a flimsy excuse as to why I couldn't go out. Once they started sending me on the trips, that part was easy. It's hard to have a personal life when you travel three weeks out of a month. Most of the guys I met were ones I worked with, and I was careful about dating any of them. It's hard enough to get ahead in the corporate world without everyone talking about you behind your back. I didn't want them to imply that I slept my way to the top." She hesitated for a second, closing her eyes and taking a deep breath. *Keep going.*

"But most of them didn't make it past the second date, if they even made it to the first date. But I wanted to know what it was like, what I was missing out on, so I let one of the other girls in the office set me up with another attorney she knew. And he seemed nice and we had a lot in common, so I decided one night that I was going to just go for it and have sex. But I had to drink a lot before I could, um, do it." As she felt him tense, she laid a hand on his arm. "Don't get me wrong, it wasn't rape. I knew what I was doing, I wasn't passed out drunk, or anything like that. I just couldn't relax enough to have sex. I'd tried before...I'd get to a certain point and I'd freeze up. But even with the alcohol, all I did was just lay there..." She averted her eyes, the shame and embarrassment welling up in her again, as she remembered that night and the names she'd been called after it was over. "Let's just say the experience didn't instill any faith in my abilities to please a man and I never tried after that.

"I would remember how I felt when I was with you, how you made me feel with your touches, and I knew something was wrong, that there was something missing and I should have been able to enjoy it...no, don't say anything. I need to get this out all at once, or I may chicken out again." She felt him jerk at her admission, and she squeezed his arm to keep him quiet.

With a deep breath, she forced herself to finish. "Nothing ever came close to what we had and I wasn't willing to settle for less, I guess. Plus there was the whole issue of my childhood. I'd be with a guy, and he'd being doing all the right things, saying all the right things, but I'd have a panic attack. I'd feel like I was suffocating and I'd feel like I couldn't breathe. The last guy I was seeing, somehow he managed to stick around longer than any of the others. He was another attorney for the firm, but not in my department, so I thought it might work," she paused to collect her thoughts. "I was beginning to think *he* might be worth it and I was trying to talk myself into sleeping with him, to try trusting in someone else for a change. I knew he was getting frustrated, waiting for me...He had turned on the charm and wined and dined me when I moved back to Austin, but I froze every time he tried to...And then I found out that he was messing around when I was out of town, or even not out of town. So I broke up with him, the day of the accident. I had walked in on him with one of the paralegals from the office, in a very compromising position. I told her she could have him, told him not to bother calling me, and I walked out the door," she finished. "Four weeks later, I was discharged from the hospital and I came home to Waketon."

"And here we are," Jason whispered.

"And here we are, again," she agreed, her heart racing.

He was so quiet during all of that, what is he thinking? I shouldn't have told him. "And now I am terrified." Her heart felt like it was going to jump out of her chest.

"Of me?" he reached out and wrapped both arms around her again, and she nestled close, sighing. *At least he didn't jump up and shove me out the door.*

"Yes and no. What if we can't recapture what we had or if it all falls apart? I walked away once but it almost killed me," she admitted. "I can't go through that again."

His arms tightened around her. "Neither can I," he replied. "I can't tell you what the future holds for us, baby, but I can tell you this. I'd rather have this second chance with you than to never know and have to live with the 'what might have been's."

"Jason..." She was toying with one of the buttons on his polo shirt, so he waited, giving her the time he knew she needed to sort through her thoughts. "I need you to know that I think I made the biggest mistake of my life walking away from you, and I knew it about nine years and a half years ago, but I was too confused and ashamed to come back."

He leaned away from her, and with his finger under her chin, forced her to look up at him. "I knew it the second you walked away, but I was too hurt and angry to come after you. I wish you had trusted me enough to talk to me like this, back then. It took a long time for me to let go of that anger, Cole, but I think I can understand better now what was going through your mind and the confusion you must have been feeling. Hopefully, we'll both be better able to deal with our feelings."

He kissed her lips, and she reached up to cradle his face in her palm. He adjusted her so that she was lying across his lap. Supporting her with his left arm, his right hand was gripping her hip. She could feel the heat through her dress. She reached up and wrapped her arms around his neck, begging him to deepen the kisses without words. Soon, they were stretched out on the sofa, the front of her dress unbuttoned, and his shirt tossed to the floor. She teased the mat of dark hair on his chest with her fingertips while his fingers played at the edges of her bra and he nuzzled her neck. His body moved against her and she could feel his erection through his jeans. She shifted, allowing the contours of her body to align with his, rubbing against him. Gasping at the sudden heat pooling between her thighs, she pressed herself closer. Groaning he kissed a path down to the swell of her breasts.

"Still think we can't recapture what we had?" He whispered as he reached down and undid the front closure of her bra, parting it and looking at her.

She stiffened and he bent his head to kiss her again, keeping his left hand on her breast, not moving. She felt herself relaxing, and as he felt it, his fingers began to move on her breast. Using his fingers, he teased her nipple. His lips started retracing their earlier path down her neck, his right arm under her, holding her close to him. A moan escaped her as his lips closed over her nipple and her arms slipped around him. Her fingernails were digging into the muscles of his back. Her leg drew up and over his hip when his thigh insinuated itself between her legs. His fingers bit into her hip as he drew her up against him, letting his erection pressed against her. Her dress had ridden up her thighs, and she became aware of his hand, stroking her thigh and moving up higher, to the edge of her panties. The old familiar feeling of panic overtook her and like a bucket of ice water, extinguished the flames of desire.

"Jason..." she whispered, pushing against his chest. "Jason, I can't!"

Groaning, Jason lifted off of her, grabbing his shirt off the floor and shrugging into it as he moved over to the window and stared out at the dark water below.

She was slower to sit up, but once she did, she hurried to restore order to her clothes. Standing, she walked over to stand behind him. Not knowing what else to do, she reached and touched his shoulder. "I'm sorry..." she whispered.

He turned and took her in his arms. "No, I'm sorry. I promised you we would go as slow as you need to. And I promised *myself* I wouldn't put us in this situation. It's too damned uncomfortable." He told her as he kissed the top of her bent head. "We're going to have to be careful from now on because much more of that and I'm not sure I'll care about any promises I've made, to you or anyone else."

They stood at the window for a few minutes, just holding each other, before he stepped back. "I think I should take you home now." She nodded, retrieving her purse from the coffee table. Following him out to the truck, she climbed in when he opened the door for her. He looked over at her as he slid behind the steering wheel, noticing the stiff way she was holding herself and the tight features of her face.

"Hey." He reached over and turned her face to his. "What's wrong?" She tried to turn her head away and he was even more alarmed when her eyes began to fill with tears.

"Nicole, honey, don't cry." He slid across the seat and wrapped her in his arms. "Talk to me, baby."

"I can't. I'm too embarrassed." She sniffed. "Jesus Christ, I'm over thirty years old and I can't get past my hang-ups and make love with the one man I've been fantasizing about and comparing every other man to for over ten years!"

He pulled away from her and stared down at her and she saw her own shock mirrored on his face. "Oh my God, I can't believe I just said that." Nicole gave a shaky laugh. "So, here's the part where you decide I am too neurotic and emotionally messed up, you start the engine, drive me home and then refuse to take my calls until I get the hint and stop calling."

"As if," he told her, claiming her mouth with his own. "After a declaration like that, you aren't going anywhere," he opened his door, slid out and reached back in to pull her out. "You're staying with me tonight." He swung her up in his arms and strode back to his front door. She hid her face against his neck, while he opened the door. He carried her back to his bedroom and sat down on the bed, still holding her. "I promise, even if it kills me, I won't touch you until

93

you ask me to. But you are going to spend the night in my arms."

Nicole released a soft sob and buried her face against his shoulder. "Jason..."

"Hush. It's my turn. You're going to have to trust me, Nicole. I am not looking for a one night stand with you. I never was. If all I wanted from you was sex, I could have had you on the couch out there less than thirty minutes ago. And I sure as hell could have coaxed you into my bed ten years ago." He shifted her in his arms so that she was straddling his lap and facing him. "For your information, I am in love with you and always have been. I tried to move on, and if anyone had asked me, I would have said I was over you. But when I wouldn't marry Sara, I had to be honest with myself and admit I still loved you. Hell, I took the job here just so I'd have a chance of seeing you if you ever came to town." He gave her a soft kiss.

"Now, you can borrow one of my t shirts and a pair of shorts if you want them. I'm going to go back outside and make sure my truck is locked up and then we're going to go to sleep before I forget my good intentions and take advantage of you." He set her on her feet and stood up. He went over to his dresser and handed her the promised t shirt and shorts, pointed her in the direction of his bathroom and walked out closing the door behind him.

She scurried into the bathroom, and changed clothes as fast as she could before he came back into the room. Looking in the mirror, she groaned at the damage her tears had caused to her makeup. Spying towels and washcloths on a shelf next to the shower, she grabbed one and scrubbed her face clean. She was just stepping out of the bathroom when he gave a soft knock on the door before opening it.

"I like it." He grinned at her, taking in the t shirt, which came almost to her knees. With a shy smile, she handed over the shorts.

"I think the t shirt is long enough that I don't need these," she told him. Standing in the doorway, she waited for him to make the next move.

"Go ahead and climb into bed. I'll go change." He touched her arm as she started to step away, stopping her. When she tilted her head back to look at him, he leaned in and gave her a soft kiss. "We'll figure it out, baby. I promise," he whispered against her lips. Giving her a tender smile and a gentle push towards the bed, he moved towards the bathroom.

She was in bed with the covers pulled to her chin when he walked out of the bathroom a few minutes later, dressed only in the shorts she had handed him minus his shirt.

After turning the lights off, he climbed into the bed beside her. He turned on his side and propped himself on his elbow. Chuckling at her stiff posture, he reached over and traced the curve of her cheek with his finger, and then tucked a loose strand of hair behind her ear. "I swear I won't attack you in the night. Are you going to be able to relax and go to sleep?"

"I've never slept with anyone before," she whispered, turning her head to look at him. "I don't know..."

"Shh. Turn on your side...no, the other way." He turned her so she was facing away from him. Pulling her up against him, cradling her back to his front, he wrapped his arm around her waist. Stretching out behind her, keeping his arm above the covers, but around her middle, he nuzzled her neck. "Now, relax and go to sleep," he whispered.

She slid one of her arms out from under the covers and grabbed his hand, giving it a squeeze. "Jason?"

"Hmm?" His voice was husky with sleep.

"Thank you." She felt his lips move against her hair and he gave her hand a return squeeze. She felt herself relaxing and within minutes she was sound asleep.

CHAPTER 9

Nicole woke up early the next morning, confused for a few brief seconds about where she was. As the events of the previous night came rushing back to her, she became aware of Jason's arm around her. They were still in the same position they had been in when she fell asleep, but during the night, his leg had inserted itself between hers, and the t shirt had ridden up to her waist. Trying not to wake him, she turned over and watched him while he slept.

The sheet she had pulled up to her chin before he had climbed into the bed with her was pushed to his waist. His breathing was still slow and even. It felt so *right* to wake up in his bed with his arms around her. She let herself think about how it would feel to wake up like this, every morning, feeling safe, secure. Loved. With some hesitation, she reached out and touched her finger to his lips. It must have tickled him, because his lips twitched, but his breathing didn't change.

Confident that he was still asleep and braver than she

would have been had he been awake, she flattened her hand against his chest and ran her fingers through the mat of hair. He shifted, pulling her closer against him, and she felt the stirrings of his erection against her thigh. She moved against him, and kissed his throat. His arm tightened around her, but still he didn't wake up. Growing bolder, she pressed a series of kisses down his throat to his chest, to the nipple hidden in his chest hair.

Remembering how she had felt the night before when he had put his mouth on hers, she pressed her lips to it, and felt it harden. Pleased to know that she could evoke the same response from him that he'd gotten from her, she pressed her open mouth over his nipple and flicked it with her tongue.

And found herself flat on her back, Jason leaning over her with his weight between her legs, causing a new kind of ache to spread.

"Good morning," he whispered his voice still husky with sleep. Bending his head to capture her mouth, he grabbed her hands and held them down against the pillows on either side of her head. "What do you think you're doing?"

"I was just, um, experimenting," she whispered between kisses. She moved her hips, causing him to groan.

"Jesus, Cole." He let go of her hands to grab her hips in order to keep her from moving against him. "I'm warning you right now...if you don't stop, I'm not going to be able to." He tried to shift his hips away from her, but she hooked a leg around him to hold him still. He looked into her eyes, and she smiled, as she wrapped her arms around his neck, urging his mouth back down to hers. She ran her fingertips down his spine, and under the elastic band of the shorts.

"Cole..." Jason pulled his mouth away from hers, and grabbed the hem of her t shirt, his knuckles brushing against her stomach. "Tell me to stop right now, or there's no going back."

"There's no going back," she whispered, lifting her head to spread kisses across his chest. He yanked the t shirt up and over her head, throwing it to the floor, pressing her back into the mattress. Kissing her throat, he worked his way down to her breasts. Turning onto his side, he dragged her up against him, shoving her panties down her legs. He eased his hand between her legs and touched her. She clenched her thighs, her instincts telling her to fight the intrusion.

Murmuring to her, he again claimed her mouth with his, alternating soft, teasing kisses with deep ones, thrusting his tongue in and out, chasing hers. She relaxed, allowing him to position her leg over his hip. Feeling his finger easing back and forth, slowing moving inside of her, she felt the slickness as he readied her for what was next. His other hand was shaping her breast, and his mouth alternated between giving her kisses, and suckling her. She was moaning and begging him for release and still he pushed her higher.

She could feel his erection, through his shorts, pressing against her *there*. She was going to go mad if he didn't end the torment soon. She worked her hands under the waistband of the shorts, and reached down to stroke his erection. She gripped his hips and pulled him up against her.

"Please...Jason."

"You started it." He chuckled, leaning back and looking into her eyes, his hand still between her legs, her hand still wrapped around him.

"I'm asking you to finish it," she moaned as he again took her nipple into his mouth.

"Are you sure?" he asked one last time.

She nodded, shoving at his shorts. Jason rolled off of her long enough to kick his shorts off and then he was back, moving over her. He positioned himself between her thighs, and she wrapped her legs around him. Groaning, he tried to control his entry, not wanting to thrust too deeply too fast, so as not to hurt her.

"Jason..."She groaned, needing him to go deeper.

"Easy, baby, I don't want to hurt you. Jesus, baby, you're so tight," he clenched his jaw as he pushed a little deeper, resisting the urge to bury himself inside of her. She moaned, closing her eyes and willing her muscles to relax. He reached between them and rolled her nipple between his fingers, bending his head to flick it with his tongue. She pulled her legs up and wrapped them around his waist, and that was his undoing. He covered her mouth with his own as he thrust deep. He felt her stiffen under him, her hands coming up between them and flattening against his chest. He forced himself to hold still, pushing himself up onto his elbows.

"Cole, baby, are you okay?" he pressed a soft kiss against her lips.

"Mm hmm." She opened her eyes and looked at him. Her hands stroked his chest now, pulling him closer. She rolled her hips, feeling her muscles stretch and tighten around him. "I need..."

"I know, but I don't want to hurt you anymore than I already have." He laid his forehead against hers. "God, you are so tight. Oh, god, baby." He groaned as she moved her hips again. "If you keep doing that, I'm going to come." He warned, thrusting with slow, shallow movements, trying to allow her body time to accept him. As he felt her body relax and accept him, he began to move again, slow at first, and then faster, deeper. She felt herself losing control, reaching toward some pinnacle, racing for it, and then hurtling over the edge.

"So, what brought that on?" Jason asked some time later, laying on his back, Nicole sprawled across his chest. He had his arms wrapped around her, stroking one hand up and down her spine. Her fingers were teasing the hairs on his chest.

"I woke up and it just felt so right, being in your arms. And I realized I didn't want to keep living in the past with the 'might have beens'. I wanted you to know I trust you, and I love you."

Tightening his arms around her, he rolled, pinning her beneath him. "It felt right, to me, too," he told her, smoothing the hair back away from her face. "I thought I was going to die of a heart attack when you started touching my chest."

"You were asleep!" Nicole pushed against him. "Weren't you?"

"Nope. Not since you rolled over and started running your fingers over my lips." He grinned down at her. "I didn't want you to fly out of bed, embarrassed, so I

pretended to be asleep. I never knew you would go so far."
Bending his head, he pressed a soft kiss to her lips, then
leaned back and glanced down. "Are you sore?"

"A little." She admitted, feeling heat rush to her face.

"Too sore?" He moved against her, and she could feel
him, not quite fully erect, but getting hard.

"Shoot me if I'm ever too sore for this." She reached up
and pulled him back down to her. He laughed, turning
them again so that this time she was on top, straddling his
hips, in control, and giving him full access to her breasts. It
was a long time before either of them could think clearly
again.

"Oh, my God!" Nicole moaned, sitting up on the side of
the bed.

"Are you ok? What's wrong? Is it your back?" Jason
stuck his head out from the bathroom, where he had just
finished his shower, and watched her try to get out of bed.

"Two things, well, three actually." She pushed to her
feet and walked towards him. "First, I'm sore, not that I'm
sorry, but...well, I'm sore." Laughing, he pulled her up
against him and gave her a quick kiss.

"What are the other two things?" he asked, releasing
her and stepping back over to the sink to shave.

"Jack, Mitch, and Carly are never going to shut up
now." She met his eyes in the mirror, and then glanced
away. "And three: we didn't use birth control." She waited
a beat, and then looked back towards him. He paused with
the razor halfway to his face and met her eyes in the mirror.

"I see," he turned back to the mirror to finish shaving.

Her heart pounding, not sure what to do or think, she leaned against the wall. Grabbing a towel, he wiped the remnants of soap off his face before stepping over to stand in front of her and took her hands in his. His thumbs rubbed over her knuckles, soothing her.

"Say something," she whispered, searching his eyes.

"First, I'm sorry you're sore, but you can take a warm bath after I drop you off at the house and that should help. Second, let them, we can handle them, can't we? And third, I know, and I don't care. I love you and I plan to marry you," he leaned in and kissed her.

"Marry?" she gasped. "You still want to marry me?"

"Yup. I want the whole enchilada. You and me with a house in the country, a couple of kids, maybe some horses, and a dog," he kissed her nose. "But I am not going to pressure you. I made some promises to you last night, and I intend to keep them. But," he added as he turned around to head for his closet to get dressed, "I am not going to promise to keep my hands to myself anymore, so unless you *do* want to get pregnant, we need to decide what we are going to do. I can take care of it for the short term, but you might want to talk to your doctor."

"You are my doctor." She reminded him with a smile.

"I meant your gynecologist. I can recommend one here in town, if you want," he chuckled, as he finished getting dressed. He came back over and stood in front of her. He paused as he tucked in his shirt. "Where are you at in your cycle?"

She did some quick calculating in her head. "I'm about a week away from my period starting, I think." She blushed, looking away from him. "How..." She swallowed hard and

forced herself to look back at him. "Have you ever, I mean...
Oh God!" she groaned, feeling the heat radiating from her
cheeks.

"Easy, honey," he stepped over in front of her and put
his hands on her shoulders. "Unprotected sex is not something I do, as a rule. There have been occasions, like this
morning, but I swear I'm clean."

"Thank you," she sighed, laying her head on his chest.
"And just so you know, my one time, before this, I mean, I
made sure he used a condom, too." His lips were on her
hair.

"Now, you need to get dressed so I can take you home.
Do you want some clean shorts and a t shirt, or do you just
want to put your dress back on?" She opted for the shorts
and a t shirt and he handed them over to her and then left
her alone to get dressed. She saw her reflection in the
mirror, and couldn't help smiling at herself. There was a
light in her eyes that hadn't been there for a very long time,
and after his comment, she was beginning to think ahead to
the future she never had dared to let herself dream was
even possible.

CHAPTER 10

Nicole walked out of his bedroom and stood hesitated in the doorway to the kitchen.

"Coffee?" He held a mug out to her.

Nodding, she stepped over and reached out to take it.

He leaned in and gave her a gentle kiss before letting go of the mug. "I'm sorry we have to hurry out of here, but I have a patient scheduled for nine-thirty."

She glanced at the clock; it was already after eight.

"I can call Carly..." she started to offer, but he shook his head.

"I want to drive you home." He reached over and laid his palm against her cheek. "Are you okay? Your ribs and your back aren't bothering you, are they?"

"I'm fine." She lowered her eyes. "It's all so new. I'm not sure..." She felt him tense as her voice trailed off and her eyes flew up to his. "I mean, I'm not sure how to act. I've never had to do the morning after thing."

"Ah, well let's see if I can help you along." He reached over, took the mug of coffee out of her hand, placing it on the counter, and then pulled her into his embrace. "First, you say 'Good morning', and then you give me a kiss." He paused and she reached up and gave him a soft kiss on the lips. He smiled down at her. "Then, for future reference, you should offer to make me breakfast while I shower and get ready for the day." Laughing, she shoved at his chest and pushed him backwards.

"Since I'm the guest, you should be offering to fix *me* breakfast." She told him, picking up the coffee mug and taking another sip.

"Stay the night with me Friday, when I don't have to be at the office the next morning, and we can discuss whose job it is to make breakfast." He grabbed his bag off the counter and with a hand at her back, guided her out the door to his truck.

"So, what are your plans for today?" He asked, as he drove her back towards Mitch's and Carly's. He reached over and took her hand, holding it against his thigh while he drove.

"There's one more contract I need to finish reviewing for Jack and Mitch, and then...I don't know. Relax in a tub, maybe?" She shifted in her seat and shot him a rueful glance. "What about you?"

"Office hours until about five, and then I am on call at the hospital tonight." He gave her hand a squeeze. "This means I won't get home until late and will get paged countless times for every stubbed toe that comes into the ER and I won't get any sleep."

"Do you have to stay there?"

"No, it's not like when I was in Residency. I can have a

life now." He grinned over at her. "Are you trying to invite yourself over tonight?"

"You could call me later, and we could maybe discuss the possibilities..." She traced a circle on his thigh with her fingernail.

"Stop that." He grabbed her hand, giving her a grin. "You don't know yet what your touch does to me." He brought her hand to his mouth and pressed a kiss to her palm. "We'll have to wait and see how the day goes. It never seems to fail: I'm on call, and everyone within a five mile radius of the hospital breaks a bone. I'd hate to make plans with you and then have to cancel."

She smiled her understanding, and they rode the rest of the way in relative silence, listening to the radio.

"Damn," she muttered under her breath as they pulled up in front of the house.

"What?" Jason had opened his door and was stepping down, but turned around at her voice.

"There's a welcome party." She jerked her head towards the porch.

He glanced over and groaned. Jack, Mitch, and Carly were all enjoying their morning coffee on the front porch, and all three of them were grinning. "Can't I just come to work with you?" She slid across the seat to get out on Jason's side, buying herself a few extra seconds.

"I wouldn't get any work done. I'd be too busy trying to get you into the exam room so I could live out the fantasy I had that first day you were in my clinic." He tapped the tip of her nose with his finger.

"You were fantasizing about me? I thought you hated me," she wrinkled her nose at him.

"I thought you hated *me*. I had to act tough, show you that I was over you, and all of that crap." He leaned down and kissed the tip of her nose. "Come on." He grabbed her hand and they walked up the porch steps together.

"Good morning. You two must have been up early, for him to drive over here to pick you up and take you on a drive this morning. We didn't even hear his truck," Mitch greeted them. "And out pretty late last night for us not to hear him drop you off. I like the outfit, by the way."

"Shut up." She stuck her tongue out and sat down in one of the porch chairs. "Any coffee left? He wouldn't let me finish mine."

"How barbaric," Jack handed her an empty mug from the table beside him and looked over at Jason. "You should always let a lady finish..." he grunted when Carly hit him on the shoulder, saving Jason the trouble.

"Be nice, you two," she instructed. "Jason, sit down. Can I get Maria to bring you out something to eat?"

"No, thanks, Carly. I need to get going. Unlike some people around here, I have work to do." He slapped Mitch on the back, and then leaned down and kissed Nicole. "I'll call you later." He went back down the steps to his truck, and with a small wave, drove off back down the lane.

Mitch waited until the truck was out of sight, and then turned to his cousin. "Well, looks like you two are getting along okay."

"That would be one way of putting it." Nicole agreed, taking a sip of her coffee, refusing to meet his eyes.

Jack came to her rescue, asking her if she had a few minutes to talk to him about something. She nodded and she and Jack stood up and walked inside, borrowing Mitch's office.

"What's up?"

"I brought over the contracts for you to sign to lease out those 15 acres to Paulson for winter grazing this year." He handed a stack of papers over to her.

She took them and laid them aside, looking back at him with a raised eyebrow. "You drove all the way over here this morning for a signature that isn't needed until September?"

"No, Mitch and I had some ranch business to discuss, as well."

Jack sat down in one of the armchairs, and she sat in the other, facing him. Hesitating, he glanced out the window, and then back at her. "Nicole..." his voice trailed off.

"Go ahead. Carly and Mitch had their say the other night," she resigned herself for another lecture. It shouldn't have surprised her, Jack wanting his say. They may not be related by blood, but he had a protective streak five miles wide where she was concerned.

"It isn't a secret in this family that your mother had some twisted ideas about how her marriage, and having you, held her back. But sometimes, it's worth the risks. Look at Helen and Steve, or Mitch and Carly. They gambled on love, and came out winners."

"This from the man who dates women from out of town so that he doesn't have to worry about them breathing down his neck?" Nicole pursed her lips and eyed him.

"I thought about it once, but got burned so badly, I never had the desire to try again," Jack admitted, meeting her gaze.

"When?" she asked, shocked.

"Right before I left for my tour of duty. She dropped me the first time she saw the scars and found out I wasn't going to have the deep pockets she was counting on," Jack shook his head, "It hurt for a while, made me bitter for a long while, but I moved on, a little worse for wear, but wiser."

"Oh, Jack. I never knew," Nicole laid her hand on his arm, and he covered it with his own.

"All that shit happened at the same time...getting sent off to war and then shot up, coming home to recover and getting dumped. I was just trying to survive at least one of them." He stood up and grabbed his Stetson off the table where he'd tossed it earlier and headed for the door. "I need to get to town. Don't forget to sign off on that contract."

After Jack left, she headed down the hall to her room, and ran herself a hot bath to try and soak away some of the soreness she was experiencing. She glanced at the papers he'd given her and then set them aside, to be looked at in detail after her bath. She eased herself into the tub with a slight grimace as the muscles in her thighs protested, and sighed.

What a night, she thought to herself, with a grin. A replay of the night's events went through her mind. She was still finding it hard to believe Jason wasn't high tailing it out of her life after what she revealed. Here she was, the child of a murderer, and he was still talking about forever with her. She knew they still needed to work through a few things and she needed to put more of her own past to rest. But they had a chance, a real chance, this time of making it work.

Figuring out the rest of her life wasn't going to be a

picnic, either. Jobs in and around Waketon for out-of-work attorneys were pretty scarce. She didn't need to rely on a steady paycheck, which was good, but she didn't want to burn through her portfolio or live off her family forever.

There was also the whole property thing. When her father killed himself and her mother, she inherited everything they had. The piece of land he'd owned was by far worth the most. She'd tried hard to sign it over to her uncle, but he wouldn't take it.

"It's yours, Nicole. When you're old enough to make the decision on your own, you can sell it. But while I'm your guardian, you're hanging onto it," he'd told her.

Sitting her down with his attorney, they had gone over every aspect of her inheritance. The attorney was the one who suggested they lease the land, giving her some income from it to offset taxes. Every couple of years, she debated selling the land but just could never bring herself to do it. It was the only thing she had left of her father.

She rested her head against the edge of the tub, letting the hot water soak into her abused muscles. It was time to move forward, she decided with a sigh. Time to let go of the past and put it all to rest.

CHAPTER 11

Nicole hid out in her bedroom, looking over the paperwork Jack had given her, until she was confident that Mitch would be out of the house. Heading downstairs, she found Carly in the kitchen, making out a shopping list. She set her stack of papers on the table, along with her purse, and moved over to the coffee pot, grabbing a mug and filling it, before turning to her friend.

"Hey."

"Hey, yourself. Feel better?" Carly gave her a knowing look before turning back to the spice rack.

"About a lot of things," she admitted, grinning. "Where is everyone?"

"Jack went to work, Mitch is out riding the fence line this morning, Maria is upstairs cleaning Helen and Steve's room, and you and I are here in the kitchen," Carly put down her shopping list, grabbed her glass of ice water and sat down at the table. "You cheated me out of details the last time, so you'd better spill now!"

She laughed and sat down beside Carly at the table. "We went to dinner, then he took me back to his place, and we talked." She blushed when her friend made a disbelieving sound. "*We talked*" she emphasized, and then added "before moving on to other things."

"It's the *other things* I'm interested in," Carly teased.

Nicole took a sip of her coffee before answering. "We made out on the couch for a little bit, I said no, he started to bring me home, I let it slip that I had been having fantasies about him for years and he made me spend the night in his arms, just holding me," she set her cup down on the table.

"Wow," Carly leaned in and examined her friend's face. "And nothing happened?"

"Not last night, no," Nicole looked away, blushing even more.

"You're holding out on me! What happened?"

"I woke up this morning before he did, and it felt so right to be there. And I realized I've let my mother's screwed up views rule my life long enough," Nicole felt as if her face were on fire at this point. "He woke up and, well..."

"You did it!" Carly supplied for her, grinning like a maniac. "Was he worth waiting all your life for?"

"Carly!"

"Listen, honey, I've had to listen to all the women in this town for the last few years talk about him and we have all wondered. Now I have the chance to get the goods, and I want details! You can trust me; you know I won't go around telling tales."

Blushing, Nicole fiddled with her coffee before answering. "Yes, he was worth the wait."

"So, are you going to see him tonight? What's next?"

"We didn't make any definite plans. He's on call tonight, so he said he'd call me later," she finished off her coffee. "For the first time in a *very* long time, I am letting myself think about what I want and need to be happy," she stood up and took her empty mug over to the sink. "Now, on that note, I need a small favor."

"Anything," Carly leaned back in her chair, still grinning.

"I need to borrow a vehicle, and I need to know where Mitch keeps my keys." She swallowed hard. "It's time to go deal with my past and those ghosts."

Carly stood up and walked over to her, giving her a warm hug. "Do you need me to go with you?"

"Not this time. I need to do this on my own. But thank you," she shook her head as she reached for her purse and the papers she had set down.

Carly grabbed her own purse off the counter. "Here, take the truck. You'll find the other keys in the top drawer of Mitch's desk. They're labeled," she handed a set of keys over to her.

Nicole headed to Mitch's office where she found the keys right where Carly had told her they'd be. Today was a day for new starts and she was determined to start putting the past where it belonged, once and for all. It was just a few short miles to her destination. She drove slower than normal, not in any hurry to get there. Steve had padlocked the gate to help keep out trespassers, so it was a bit of a hassle to have to stop and open the gate, drive through and then stop and get out to shut it again. She drove up the dirt road to where the house used to sit, only the slab of the foundation now standing. She sat in the truck, staring at the slab, and let the memories in for the first time since she was fifteen.

Climbing out of the truck, she moved over to the slab and sat down on what used to be the front porch steps. The house had been destroyed by a tornado five years after her parents' deaths. She'd been relieved when she'd found out; at least she didn't have to feel guilty for not wanting to live there.

She couldn't remember ever being close to her mother. Even as a very young child, she knew to either go to her aunt or her father with any problems. Her mother was too busy getting her hair done, or her nails, or going shopping, to be bothered with a child's problems. There had been many mornings, even before she was old enough for school, she could remember riding over to her aunt's house with her father. Since he was the foreman for Uncle Steve, it had been easy for him to drop her off in the mornings and then bring her home at night.

She and her father had been close. He used to sit with her on these very steps, she remembered. Everything she knew about baseball, he had taught her. Every milestone, every sporting event, every school event she ever had, he was there for her. She still missed him, she realized. Even as hurt and angry as she was for what he'd done to her world, she missed him.

Nicole pushed herself to her feet and climbed back into the truck, driving out across the range, remembering and reliving her youth. She drove out to the creek, where it widened and formed an area deep enough for swimming and fishing, remembering when her father had taught her to do both of those there. There was an outcropping of rocks and a small grove of trees that offered some shade from the heat of the August sun. Making her way to the rocks, she pulled herself up onto one of them and sat down, watching the water as it rippled from the slight breeze.

She leaned back on her elbows and studied the terrain around her, contemplating her choices. Option number one was to stay in Waketon, build a new house on this land, and see what happened between her and Jason. For option number two, she could sell the land and move back to the city. That option would include finding a new job, continuing the life of the dedicated career woman that she had so carefully constructed, and not risk losing her heart any more than she already had.

She thought back to the conversation she had had with Mitch a few nights ago. "Figure out what you want," he said, as if it were the easiest thing in the world to do. Of course, he'd included in that conversation that she could either learn from her past of be miserable like her mother.

"I wish I knew what to do, Daddy," she murmured, looking out over her father's beloved land, with a heavy sigh. "I hope I don't disappoint you. I just want to be happy." Only the sounds of the birds in the trees answered her.

CHAPTER 12

Nicole made her way back to the ranch around lunchtime, groaning when she saw Mitch's truck parked in front of the house. She parked beside it and climbed down, grabbing her stack of papers off the seat. Mitch and Carly were both in the kitchen, eating lunch.

"There you are. I was starting to get worried," Carly greeted her. "Pull up a chair, make yourself a sandwich. Where were you?"

"I drove over to my property, drove around for a while, tried to put to rest those old ghosts we talked about," Nicole replied as she made herself a thick sandwich, and piled some potato chips on her plate. "And then I started making some plans. Nothing I'm willing to share yet," she cautioned as both of them opened their mouths. "I still have a lot to think about."

"Jason called, he said he try again later, but asked me to let you know his day is shaping up to be a killer, so he may not be able to see you tonight." Mitch told her, noting the slight blush. "Three nights in a row. Getting serious, are we?"

"We'll see." She evaded. "Since Jack was here this morning, do you still need me to go over those stock contracts with you?"

"Actually, yes. He said if you didn't mind, he'd appreciate it. He said he's pretty swamped over at the office and it'd be doing him a huge favor, and he's not just throwing you a bone. His words, not mine." Mitch assured her, when she raised an eyebrow. "I'm going to go into my office now and catch up on a few things. Come on in when you finish your lunch." Mitch pushed back from the table and stood up, pausing beside his wife's chair to give her a tender kiss.

"Are you sure you're okay?" Carly asked, after he left the room.

"I am," she nodded and smiled over at her friend. "For the first time in a long time, I am." She, too, pushed back from the table and stood up. "I am going to go and try to explain those contracts to Mitch in simple terms." She grinned at her friend, started to walk out of the room, and then turned back. "I, uh, also need the name and number of your gynecologist." Laughing with delight, Carly dug a card out of her wallet and handed it over.

"Thanks," Nicole muttered, feeling her cheeks flaming once again as she walked down the hall to her cousin's office.

It didn't take long to go over the contracts with Mitch; they were the standard contracts he and his dad tended to use when they were buying and selling their cattle. She had made a few notations where she thought they should change a few things, so Mitch noted them for his father to look at when he got back on Sunday before they signed them.

"Thanks, Nicole. We owe you for this. Jack's reputation has grown so much and so fast in the area, he's pulling in more clients than he can handle. You reviewing the contracts for him helped."

She grinned over at him. "I was happy to do it, you know that. You sure you understand the changes I suggested though?"

"Yup." Mitch nodded.

"Good. Then I need a favor. I need to borrow your truck again."

"Anytime. Where you headed to now?" Mitch tossed over a set of keys.

"Town. If Jason calls, tell him to call me on my cell." Nicole wrote her Austin cell phone number down on a pad of paper and pushed it across to him. "I'll be back later," she grabbed the keys and headed out the door.

Forty-five minutes later, she pulled up in front of Jack's office and headed inside. No one was seated in the outer office, but she could hear the low rumble of Jack's voice from his office. She stuck her head around the door jamb to let him know she was there, and he caught the movement out of the corner of his eye. He motioned her in, and covered the mouthpiece with his hand. "What's up?"

She indicated the stack of papers she was carrying. "I need to discuss some stuff with you." She told him. He nodded and took his hand away from the mouthpiece.

"Look, I don't think that is a decision you should be making lightly. Let me do some research and I can get back to you on..." he paused to look at his calendar. "I'll call you before noon on Monday to let you know what I find out. Okay?"

Hanging up the phone, he turned his attention her. "Have a seat. Can I get you anything? Stacy is on vacation this week, but I'm pretty sure there are still a few cold drinks in the fridge," he offered.

"No, I'm fine," she handed the papers over to him. "I signed off on these, and wrote a couple of notes down for you about a couple of changes I'd like to look into."

"You didn't have to get these back to me today," Jack took the papers and put them off to one side. "Everything okay?"

"Everything's great. I just have a few errands to run here in town, so I thought I'd go ahead and drop those off for you."

"Uh-huh. Would one of those errands be to head over to the hospital, by any chance?"

"Maybe." She grinned at him.

"Tell Jason I said he owes me a bottle of whiskey," Jack chuckled. "He'll know what I'm talking about."

Nicole stopped by the bank and talked to the account manager there to get some information and then she did swing by the hospital to try and surprise Jason, but he was in surgery. She made a quick stop at the drugstore and was headed for home when her cell phone chirped and she frowned at the display when she recognized the number on it.

"Hello?"

"Nicole! It is so good to hear your voice. How are you feeling?" Her former boss's voice boomed in her ear, causing her to wince.

"I'm fine, Robert. How are you?"

"Good, good. Nicole, we're in a bit of a pickle, though. What would it take to get you back here?"

It was a good thing no one else was on the road. She hit the brakes and swerved over onto the shoulder. "Excuse me?"

"We need you to come back." Robert repeated, cutting straight to the chase. She could picture him at his desk, in his office, feet up in the corner, phone to his ear, and an unlit cigar in the ashtray, confident that she wouldn't turn him down. "We can't bring you in as a full partner but that would be foreseeable in a year or so. Otherwise, we are willing to meet any demands you might have."

"Robert..."

"Shall we say Monday at eleven? You can think about your terms over the weekend, and have plenty of time to drive up here from that little town you've been hiding yourself in." Robert ignored whatever it was she had been about to say, and she found herself agreeing to the appointment, and hanging up.

Stunned, she sat there for a few minutes, trying to think it all through. She checked her mirrors and then pulled back out onto the road and headed for home, needing to talk to Jason.

But it was after ten o'clock that night before they were able to talk. "I'm sorry, sweetheart. I got pulled into three surgeries, and had a few patients in the office I couldn't reschedule. But I thought about you all day," he told her when she answered the phone.

"I thought about you, too," Nicole admitted, her stomach fluttering as his deep voice washed over her. "Where are you now?"

"In my condo, sitting out on the deck, enjoying the view. I miss you. What did you do today?"

"I reviewed the contracts with Mitch and spent some time with Jack, going over some leases he wrote up for me on my property. Oh, I almost forgot. He asked me to remind you that you owe him a bottle of whiskey. What's that about?" she asked him as he laughed.

"I'll tell you all about it someday," he promised, groaning. "Listen, babe, I am wiped out, and I have to see all of those patients I cancelled today, tomorrow. Tomorrow's Friday. Why don't you pack a bag and stay with me for the weekend?"

"Jason..."

"No pressure. But I want to spend time with you, alone, away from your crazy family."

"That sounds like a great idea," she agreed.

"Then borrow a truck and meet me at my place at six tomorrow night. I'll grill," he suggested.

"I do need to talk to you, though."

"I promise, we'll talk," he yawned.

"Ok. I'll be there at six. Go get some sleep," she instructed, hanging up the phone. Was it really only 24 hours ago that she'd fallen asleep in his arms?

The call from her former boss weighed heavy on her mind. She hadn't told anyone else about it, wanting to talk to Jason first. In her head, she could still hear every word her mother had ever had to say about giving up your own identity for a man, but her heart was beating out a different message. She sat down in the chair by her window and looked out at the stars. But they didn't have any answers to offer her either.

CHAPTER 13

"You're here and bearing gifts!" Jason opened the door as soon as she knocked the next evening and took the cake she held.

"When I told Maria you were cooking dinner for me, she whipped this up. She said it's one of your favorite desserts," Nicole followed him into the kitchen.

He turned around after putting the cake on the counter and pulled her into his arms. "You're my favorite dessert," he growled, his mouth hovering over hers. "God, I missed you yesterday," he proved it with a deep kiss and she let her bag drop to the floor. He eased back, eyes on her face, searching for any signs of doubt. "I could smell your perfume on my pillow last night and it drove me crazy."

"I missed you, too," she admitted with a shy smile, tilting her head back. "You sounded so tired last night." Her eyes roamed over his face.

"I was. Being woken up out of a sound sleep at five am, by a woman obsessed with my body, and then having to see patients, perform surgeries...I was beat." He leaned in and gave her another kiss that had her weak in the knees.

"Here, let me take your bag," he grabbed her overnight bag and took it into the bedroom. When he came back to the kitchen, he grabbed her hand and led the way out to his deck.

"I know I promised to grill, but I ran out of time. Do you still like pizza?" He indicated the box on the table.

"I love pizza." She confirmed, sitting down in the chair he held out for her.

"We'll grill tomorrow night," Opening the box, he held it towards her, allowing her the first piece. "So, what have you been doing the past couple of days?"

"Well, I made an appointment with Doctor Lawrence for next week, and finished reviewing those contracts for Mitch and went over them with him, so that he can go over them with Uncle Steve. I had a meeting with Jack. And now I'm here with you," she took a bite of her pizza.

"And for that I'm very thankful," he leaned across the table and gave her a soft kiss. She smiled back at him before asking "So, what's this about a bottle of whiskey between you and Jack?"

"A bet he and I made once. I was feeling pretty sorry for myself, and he had a bottle of whiskey, which I think he had one drink out of before I finished the rest. We had a stupid bet, which I guess he's now claiming to have won," he grinned at the memory. "And that's all I'm telling for now."

"You finished off a bottle of his whiskey and he let you live? He's slipping in his old age," Nicole shook her head. "I'm going to have to talk to him about that."

"Ha ha. Watch who you're calling old, little girl," he frowned at her and she stuck her tongue out at him.

"Oh, that's right. You're pushing forty, aren't you?" she batted her eyelashes at him.

"Is it an issue?" he asked, his tone serious now.

"What, that you're a few years older than me?" she laid her pizza down on the plate and cocked her head to the side. "Why would it be an issue?"

"Don't get mad at me..."

"Explanations that start with *that* are never good," she raised her eyebrows but didn't say anything else.

"I looked up the old stories about your parents. Your dad was quite a few years older than your mom."

Shocked, she sat back. "When...? I mean, why?" she shook her head.

"Last night, after we got off the phone. I surfed the 'net for a while," his hand wrapped around hers on the table. "And because I wanted to know more details."

She huffed out a breath and withdrew her hand from his, pushing back from the table. Moving over to the deck railing, she watched the small boats in the water. The grip she had on the deck's railing had her knuckles turning white. The noises behind her told her he was cleaning up the pizza and then he came up behind her and wrapped his arms around her waist, kissing her neck.

"Don't be mad," he implored.

"I'm not mad," she denied, allowing him to wrap his arms around her. Her head settled against his shoulder and they watched the boats on the water.

"If you're not mad, then what are you?"

"I'm not sure, to be honest." *Deep breaths, you already told him the worst of it and he's still here,* she reminded herself.

"So what did you find out?" somehow, her voice remained calm.

"Not much more than what you'd already told me, other than their ages. Your dad was a lot older than your mom."

"Almost fifteen years," she agreed, letting go of the railing and placing her hands on top of his. "They met through my aunt and uncle. I don't know what he saw in her, or why she agreed to marry him. She made all of us miserable."

"And she just left that day? No note or anything?"

"I had spent the day at the lake with a bunch of friends. The house was empty when I got home," she closed her eyes at the pain that was surging through her with the memories. "We always left notes on the kitchen counter and there wasn't one. I had no clue," she swallowed hard. "Uncle Steve said someone called Dad around noon and he'd taken off, saying he had personal business with mom," she gave a harsh laugh.

"I'm sorry, babe," he kissed the top of her head.

Turing into his arms, she laid her head on his chest, hearing the muffled sound of his heart beating. "Just tell me you're sticking with me."

"Oh, I'll stick," his hands rubbed up and down her back, trying to soothe and comfort.

"Where do we go from here?" she asked, leaning back to look at him.

"Nothing's changed," he assured her with a lingering kiss. "You alright?"

"Getting there. I just have this great, big wall of confusion, insecurity and uncertainty, with a few doubts trying to creep in."

He threaded his fingers through her hair, massaging her scalp. "Would it help if I told you that I love you?"

"It does help, thank you. I love you, too," her arms went up to curl around his neck, urging his head down for a soft kiss. "But this is all so new to me."

"Come on." He led her into the house and sat down on the couch, pulling her down to sit in front of him, between his legs, and started massaging her shoulders. "Now, talk it out. What are you confused about?"

"What *aren't* I confused about, that would be easier to answer," she answered. "I've gone from thinking you hated me for what I did, to discovering you love me, in less than 72 hours. I have to decide what I want to do with my life, and what that means for us, if there is an 'us'..."

He pulled her back against him and tipped her chin up so she could see his face. "There is most certainly an '*us*'. If that's one of the points you are 'uncertain' about, you can just check it off your list. I told you the other night I am not letting you go this time."

She offered a hesitant smile before sitting back up, and he continued the massage. "Well, then there's my land..."

"What land? You mentioned something last night about property," he kissed the back of her neck.

"The land my father left me. I've never done anything with it, well, except rent it out for grazing to area ranchers. The house and barn were wiped out by a tornado a few years ago, but I own about twenty acres of prime ranch land," she sighed as his lips started caressing the area below her ear. "I can't think..."

"Don't think," his voice was a whisper against her ear, as he sucked her earlobe into his mouth. His hands were under her shirt and were making their way up to her breasts. She groaned, arching her back and turning her neck to allow better access. With a growl, he turned her so that she was facing him, her knees on either side of his thighs, straddling him. Her shirt was yanked up and over her head, tossing it to the floor.

"Jason...Oh, God!" she brought her hands up to his head, gripping handfuls of his hair, trying to guide him as he trailed kisses down her neck.

"Is this what you need, baby?" he whispered, his tongue tracing the edge of her bra cup. The clasp was undone and he was pushing the straps down her arms. "Or maybe this?" He brought one hand up between them, his fingers teasing her nipple.

She gave a little cry as he bent his head, taking her nipple into his warm mouth.

"Do you like that?" Fitting her against him, he let her feel his own arousal. Unfastening her jeans, he traced the edge of her panties, around to her back. He eased his hands down to her buttocks, inside of her jeans and pulled her even closer.

"I've been hard all day, just thinking about you," he murmured against her neck, kissing his way back to her lips, moving her against him, making her own ache almost unbearable.

"Jason, please..." she groaned, grabbing fistfuls of his

shirt, twisting it in her hands, while his mouth returned to her breast and resumed their torment.

"Tell me what you need," he instructed, his mouth inches from hers.

"I need you." She arched against him, trying to ease the ache between her legs. He stood up and carried her into the bedroom, his hands gripping her buttocks as her legs wrapped around his waist. If they'd already been naked, he would have been inside of her.

He laid her on the bed, and pushed himself away and yanked off the rest of her clothes, and then his own. "Next time, you can undress me," he whispered, as he joined her on the bed. He caught her mouth with his and kissed her. His hand went between her legs, feeling her readiness for him, as he kissed his way down her throat, to her breasts. "Are you still sore?" he asked, probing with first one finger, then two. The sounds of how ready she was reached her own ears.

"Some, but I don't care!" she panted, her hand stroking him. "Jason, please! I can't wait."

"First, let me show you..." he removed his hand, bent over her, and replaced his fingers with his tongue. She thought she was going to fly off the bed. She muffled her scream with her fist.

She was aware of him moving back up her body, covering her with kisses. Entering her with one, hard thrust, she moaned.

"Are you okay?" he brushed the hair back from her face, and she opened her eyes.

"As long as you don't stop, I will be." She assured him,

smiling. He started moving within her, and she could feel every inch of him. The tension started to build within her, and once again she felt herself riding the waves. It was a long time before either of them said anything else.

CHAPTER 14

Nicole woke up early, and lay in bed beside jason, studying his relaxed features. He was sprawled on his stomach, taking up most of the bed. She realized that she still hadn't told him about the potential job in Austin. Not wanting to wake him, she eased out of the bed. She found his robe in the bathroom and slipped it on, tying it tight around her waist and moved out to the living room.

She had meant to tell him about the job last night, but they had gotten sidetracked when he started kissing her. She blushed, remembering everything they had done with each other in the bedroom. He was a very generous lover, and had encouraged her to experiment to find out what *he* liked. She had been hesitant at first to take the lead, but Jason was patient, and her confidence at being able to please him was growing.

Suddenly, his arms wrapped around her from behind and she gave a startled cry, and then relaxed against him. "Good morning," he whispered against her neck, nuzzling her. "I woke up and you were gone. For a minute, I was afraid I had dreamed the whole thing."

"I couldn't sleep, and I didn't want to wake you, you were so tired the other day..." She turned in his arms and laid her head on his chest. "We need to talk, and you can't distract me this time."

"Okay." He kissed the top of her head. "How about we make breakfast and we can talk while we eat?" he dropped his arms and led her into the kitchen. He put her in charge of toast and coffee, while he whipped up omelets for both of them.

"So you do know how to cook," she teased, watching him.

"I learned out of self-preservation. I hate cold cereal, and eating out gets expensive, even on a doctor's salary," he grinned as he slid the omelets out of the frying pan and onto plates. While she carried the plate of toast and the coffee pot to the table, he brought over the omelets.

"So, now that my mouth and hands are busy with food, talk to me," he instructed as she poured them both cups of coffee. He watched while she measured out sugar, and then added cream. "Nicole?"

"My former boss called on Thursday," she began, glancing up at him from under her eyelashes, and then away. "He's invited me to come to Austin on Monday to talk about my job. They, uh, they want me back, desperately, from the way he sounded. He said I could pretty much write my own ticket back in, that it could lead to partner in a year or so."

He set down his fork and studied her. "I thought you didn't want that lifestyle any more," he reminded her.

"I know, but..." she shrugged. "They *want* me. They're begging me to come back. And I could make *partner* in a year!" she met his gaze. "I've worked my whole life to get to this point."

"What about us? You said you couldn't just walk away this time."

"I'm not walking away. Austin is only a couple of hours away. We could make it work," she pointed out.

"How? I have a practice to run here, I'm on call at least one night a week and every third weekend. You told me yourself you traveled at least three out of four weeks a month. How could we make it work?"

"I don't know right now, but there has to be a way!" she looked over at him, near tears. "Jason, please, try to understand." This wasn't going the way she'd wanted it to, or had hoped it would. It was going exactly the way she'd feared it would.

"I'm sorry, Nicole, but I don't. You told me, just a couple of days ago, how unhappy you were with your job. And now, you want to go back to it? What about us? Are you just going to walk away again?"

"You told me during that same conversation that you wouldn't have asked me to give up my dreams ten years ago! But here you sit, doing just that! I want to make it work, Jason. I do. But you have to be willing to meet me halfway." She pushed back from the table and stood up. "I have to go." She turned and ran to the bedroom, shutting the door. Even though Jason hadn't followed her she grabbed her overnight bag and stepped into the bathroom, locking the door. She dressed and walked out to the living room, grabbing her purse and keys off of the table where she had set them the night before. She paused and looked into the kitchen, where he was still sitting.

"Goodbye, Jason," she whispered. He wouldn't even look at her. She bit her lip to hold the sobs inside and rushed from the condo, slamming the door on her way out.

CHAPTER 15

Nicole let herself into the ranch house and tried to make her way to her bedroom, but Carly was already up and came out of the kitchen. "Nicole, honey, are you okay?" She stepped forward. Nicole took one look at her friend and the dam broke, her sobs breaking free.

"What happened?" Carly took her friend into her arms and patted her on the back, leading her to her room.

"My former boss called the other day, they want me back. I told Jason about it, and he doesn't want me to go and talk to them." She reached over to the nightstand and grabbed the box of tissues. "He doesn't think it would work between us if I go back to Austin."

"Do you want to go back?" Carly asked her.

Nicole shrugged her shoulders. "I don't know any more, but I want to see what they have to offer. I need to make sure I'm doing the right thing for myself. My life has been ruled by mom's ideas for so long, and now I'm finally ready to listen to my heart, and look what that gets me!"

"Oh, sweetie. I'm sorry. Men are dogs," Carly hugged her. "Maybe once he calms down, and thinks about it..."

"But that's just it, Carly. He sat there and told me that he loved me, that we would go slow, that I made the *assumption* the last time that he would ask me to choose between him and a job. He even mentioned marriage," her voice broke on that thought and she paused to get control of her emotions. "And then as soon as I told him that there was a chance I could go back to work and my job in Austin, he started throwing out reasons it wouldn't work between us."

"Do you want me to send Mitch over there to kick his ass?" Carly asked, rubbing her friend's shoulder.

"Send Jack along for good measure," she agreed, laughing through her tears. "Oh, Carly, what am I going to do?"

Carly pushed herself to her feet. "I think you should give yourself, and Jason, some space. Drive yourself up to Austin today, check into a hotel, and just chill until Monday morning. Do all the stuff in Austin you like to do, just for yourself. Don't let yourself think about him, or the job, or anything except what you want. Then go to your meeting with a clear head. Don't make any promises to them. Make them wait for your answer. Leave 'em guessing." Carly smiled down at her friend. "My car has almost a full tank of gas. You can pack a bag and head out, if you want to," she offered.

"But Helen and Steve..."

"Their flight gets in at eight o'clock tomorrow night. I can explain everything to them, and you can talk to them later. Helen will understand." Carly interrupted. "So?"

She looked down at her hands and nodded. "I guess the alternative is to sit here and feel sorry for myself." She stood up. "Thanks, Carly."

"Hey, I cried on your shoulder often enough when Mitch and I had all that trouble. Go take care of yourself for a change." Carly headed for the door. Nicole took a quick shower and packed a bag. She checked her cell phone for messages before realizing she'd never given Jason her number. She found Carly in the living room and got the car keys from her. With a quick hug and a promise to call, she was out the door and on her way back to Austin.

CHAPTER 16

Nicole spent the next two days in austin. She did what Carly had suggested she do. She took care of herself. The salon where she always got her hair done had openings, and her stylist was willing to fit her in. Taking advantage of their spa services, she also treated herself to a massage and a manicure. On Sunday, she spent the day driving around to all of her favorite places. She spent a couple of hours at Lady Bird Lake, sitting on a park bench watching everyone pass by. She walked around one of the malls for a couple of hours, splurging on a couple of new negligées, and a few sets of matching bras and panty sets. She started to wonder if Jason would ever see her in them, but forced her mind away from anything related to *him*.

After wandering around the city for hours, she made her way back downtown to her hotel. Not wanting to be around anyone, she ordered room service for dinner and rented a movie. Her cell phone chirped a little after nine-thirty with an incoming call, and seeing that it was the phone number for the ranch, she answered.

"Nicole, honey, it is so good to hear your voice!" Aunt Helen's soft voice came across the line. "I've been so worried about you, but we couldn't get leave the humanitarian relief group short-handed, and Mitch and Jack kept assuring us that you were doing so well...You are doing well, aren't you?"

"Hi, Aunt Helen. Yes, I am fine, now. Mitch and Carly took good care of me. I'm sorry I wasn't there to welcome you both home."

"Carly filled me in on what's been happening. If your mother were still here, I'd kick her in the shins for the twisted views drummed into you. And that Jason. I thought he had more sense..." She could hear her uncle saying something in the background, and her aunt's soft laughter in response. "Listen, honey, we just got in and it has been a long couple of days. I just needed to hear your voice for myself, make sure you were okay. You take all the time you need there in Austin, but promise me you will come back down here, soon."

"I will, Aunt Helen. I am only going to stay another day or so. I promise." She said goodbye to her Aunt, spoke to Carly for a minute, and then hung up the phone. Not interested in the movie she'd rented, she turned it off, then shut the lights off and stretched out in the bed, but it was a long time before she was able to fall asleep.

She got up the next morning and went downstairs to the hotel's restaurant for breakfast. She lingered over coffee, watching all the businessmen and women cutting through the lobby on the way to their different offices.

Just a few short months ago, she had been one of those people, walking around without paying attention to her surroundings, oblivious to life. And depending on how things went today, she could be one of those people again soon.

Checking her watch, she stood up and made her way back upstairs to her room. She showered, and then styled her hair into a very business-like French twist. She applied her makeup with a careful hand, and then dressed in her business suit. Although she was only a few blocks from the office building, she was going to grab a taxi to give her a lift. It wouldn't do to appear wilted when you were trying to play hardball. Giving her reflection one last glance in the full length mirror, she grabbed her purse and attaché case and headed for the lobby.

The taxi dropped her off in front of the building, and she stood there for a few minutes, looking up at it.

"Nicole?" A voice called from behind her, and she turned. "It *is* you. Wow, you look great! We were all so worried about you!" Megan, one of the other attorneys she'd worked with walked up to her. "I was so excited when Robert told us that he was going to call and try and entice you back into the fold." Megan gave her a quick hug. "Come on, I'll walk up with you. I'll be in on the meeting, you know. Now, how are you doing?"

"I'm doing well, according to my doctor. He even said I could return to work as long as I don't fly." She ignored the tiny pang of regret she felt as she referred to Jason. "So, what's been going on here?"

Megan passed along the idle office gossip as they rode the elevator up to the firm's floor. They stepped off the elevator and Megan turned to go to her office. "It's great to have you back. I look forward to working with you again."

She was gone before Nicole had a chance to correct her. Shaking her head, she smoothed down her skirt and walked over to the receptionist's desk.

"Miss Winters! It's so good to see you!"

"Hi, Susan. Robert is expecting me, I believe."

"Yes, ma'am." Susan picked up the intercom, pressed a button and announced that Nicole had arrived. A minute later, Robert strode down the hallway to greet her. He led her back to her office. "I scheduled all of the partners and a few senior associates to meet with you, but I wanted to meet with you in private first." He told her, indicating for her to sit in one of the chairs across from his desk. "First, let me say how sorry I am that I did not listen to you when you came to me with your concerns about Peter Daniels being promoted. Quite honestly, I thought you were just being a sore loser, for lack of a better term. But within a short amount of time, it became quite clear that he was not worthy of the promotion. And when one of our biggest clients threatened to leave, well, I had to take action."

"Which client?" She let out a low whistle when Robert told her. "What happened?"

"Complete incompetence, that's what. He almost cost the client their entire business because he couldn't be bothered to think ahead or review contracts before signing off on them. Careless mistakes and incompetence," Robert reiterated, standing up. "Let's go over to the boardroom so you can greet everyone, and then we'll go have lunch and discuss your terms."

Nicole followed him down the hallway to the boardroom. She greeted all of the partners, and sat down in the chair Robert held out for her, and the meeting began.

Four hours later, she stepped through the glass doors of the office building and out onto the sidewalk. Her head was pounding from the information that had been shared, and the offer that had been made. Not only were they offering the promotion, but a substantial increase in pay, and she could restructure the department at her discretion. Travel would be at a minimum, Robert had assured her. He had looked surprised when she told him she needed time to think it over. They had expected her to jump at the chance to come back.

She started to walk back to her hotel, her mind turning the offer over and over in her head. Her cell phone rang as she was letting herself back into her room. "Hello?" She grabbed it out of her attaché case as she struggled with the key card.

"How'd it go?" Carly asked as soon as she answered.

"It was good. They want me back and are willing to meet any demands I have." She gave her a brief rundown of the meeting and named the salary they'd offered her. "I guess I have some thinking to do," she finished on a sigh.

"I guess so." Carly agreed with a laugh. "Listen, I was just calling to let you know we were all thinking about you and we're here if you need us. And also, I know you told Helen you'd be home sometime this week, but you need to make sure it's by Thursday. She wants to throw a party, welcome herself home."

"It's on my calendar," she assured her, saying goodbye and hanging up. She shed her business suit and put on her jeans and t shirt. Grabbing a pen and a notepad, she sat down at the table next to the window. Staring out at the skyline, she tapped the pen against the paper, thinking of all the pros and cons of taking this job. She always thought better when she made lists, and this was a decision she couldn't afford to screw up.

She finished the list and tossed her pen down on the table. Her eyes scanned the list and she knew what she had to do. Her decision made, she grabbed the phone book off the table, and started making phone calls. Both groups of people she wanted to meet with were free the next day, so she scheduled the appointments and then called her family to let them know she would be staying in Austin for at least another day.

CHAPTER 17

Thursday morning, nicole left austin and headed back to Waketon. She was about halfway there when her cell phone rang, the display showing Jack's name and number. Surprised he was calling now after almost a week of silence from him, she hit the button for the speaker and answered the call. Then again, he always had been able to know, even from half a continent away, when she just needed to be left alone to think things through.

"What's up?" She answered.

"Hey, kid, where are you?" He asked her. "We're having a party tonight, and they're starting to place bets as to whether or not you'll show up."

"Which side did you bet on, that way I'll know whether or not to show?" She teased him with a laugh.

"I always bet on you, you know that. You won't disappoint Helen." Jack told her. "Seriously, where are you? I expected you back yesterday."

"Relax, Jack. I'm fine. I had a few things I needed to

wrap up that I couldn't take care of on Tuesday, and the last meeting ran late yesterday. I was too tired to make the drive. I left Austin a little over an hour ago."

"Good. Stop by my office on your way in. I'd like to talk to you about something I've been kicking around in my head." Jack told her, hanging up. Shaking her head at his abruptness, she tossed her cell phone on the seat beside her. An hour and a half later, she parked the car in Jack's parking lot and headed inside his office.

"Hey. You okay?" Jack met her at the door and gave her a warm hug, before holding her away from him so he could look her over.

"I'm fine," she assured him, rolling her eyes.

"Carly said the interview went well and that they were begging you to come back," Jack led the way into his office, offering her a choice of coffee or soda. She gave him the highlights of the offer she had received.

"Wow. Tough decision!" he whistled when she finished, studying her face across the desk. "So, do you know what you're going to do?"

She sighed and leaned back in the chair, stretching her legs out in front of her. "I'm still thinking it through. I don't want to rush into anything, no matter which way I decide," she told him, meeting his gaze. "So, what did you need to see me about? You sounded so mysterious!"

"I don't want you to say anything right now, I want you to think about this, give it some serious thought," he waited for her nod her agreement. "I need to hire a partner for my practice. I know Mitch mentioned to you the other day how my reputation has grown; he wasn't kidding. It seems like everybody not only here in our county, but in the next five counties, are starting to come to me for everything from estate planning to ranching matters, family matters, and your typical DWI's. I need help, Nicole, or I'm going to have to start turning people away."

"What about hiring a paralegal?" She tilted her head to the side, her heart rate speeding up a bit as she considered where he might be going with this conversation. Jack shook his head at her suggestion.

"That would be a Band-Aid over a ruptured artery, so to speak. I need someone who can cover in court, if need be. I need someone that I would trust with my own family, with my own life. People are going to walk in that door and expect to work with me. I need to be able to say that if I can't work with them myself, the person who will be, my partner, is the next best thing. If you joined me, I could say it and mean it. Anybody else, they'd have to earn that trust from me, and that would take time. And you know how people are in communities like this; that trust is not going to come easy; it could take a few generations.

"I had planned on talking to you about this over the weekend, and then Jason had to go and pull his stunt on you, history repeating itself and all that crap. And once Carly told me why you were up in Austin, I wasn't about to throw this out there before your old firm hit you with their offer. You needed to hear their offer up front, with a clear conscience."

He came around the desk and leaned against the corner. "You've worked your ass off for the last six years to get to this spot, Nicole. I know better than anyone out there exactly how hard you *have* worked to get here. So, if that job is what you want, then you need to take it, and you show those assholes how big of a mistake they made by not promoting you six months ago, like they should have. Don't let anyone stand in your way—not Jason with his guilt trips, your mother with her taunts from beyond the grave, and certainly not me.

"But if you're ready for a change, and you'd like to come home for good, my offer is solid. I can't offer you the six figure salary they're offering in Austin, but you can have a corner office and your name on the door as a partner," he teased, "but best of all, you'd be home with the family."

He reached out his hand and pulled her to her feet. "You're my best friend and I love you. I would love for you to come home and practice law with me. But above all, I just want you to be happy," he held her by the shoulders and held her gaze. "You have two solid offers on the table. Think about them. I'm not going to pressure you with mine and I haven't mentioned it to anyone, so no one else will be trying to influence you either. I'm in no rush to get an answer. Okay?" he waited for her to nod before he pulled her back into his arms for a warm hug.

"Now, Helen has been chomping at the bit all week, waiting for you to come home so that she could make sure for herself that you are okay," Jack gave her a gentle shove in the direction of the door. "I'll see you tonight. Think about my offer for as long as you need."

She paused at the doorway of his office, glancing back over her shoulder and giving him a brief smile. She headed back out to her car and made her way back to the ranch, mulling over what Jack had just offered her. Halfway to the ranch she realized she hadn't said a single word to Jack since he'd started laying out his offer.

Twenty minutes later, Nicole parked the car in front of the house, and Aunt Helen came running down the porch steps to see her.

"Oh, honey, it's so good to see you!" Helen grabbed her niece and pulled her into her arms. "We so wanted to return home, but they needed us on the mission trip and the boys said you were doing fine and Carly swore she was making sure you were doing the rehab. But I still felt so guilty not coming back!" Helen led her up the steps and into the house.

Laughing, she returned her aunt's enthusiastic greeting. "I felt guilty enough over Mitch and Carly cancelling their vacation. I'm glad you and Steve stayed with the rest of the missionaries." They walked into the living room and Nicole sat down on the couch, Helen next to her. "I'm sorry I wasn't here on Sunday."

"Oh, honey, don't worry about that! Carly and Mitch filled us in. I'm just happy you're here now." Helen told her, giving her another hug and then held her niece by the shoulders as she looked at her. "Now, how are you *really* doing? And remember, Carly has a temper and has been threatening various body parts of our young friend Jason." Helen grinned at her niece.

She sighed and closed her eyes. "I don't know anymore, Aunt Helen. I think I'm falling in love with him, all over again, but he hurt me. I'm having enough trouble figuring out what I want to do with my life, where I want to live, if I want to continue working. I didn't need this mess thrown on top of it."

Helen wrapped her arm around her shoulders and gave her a reassuring squeeze. "I know, sweetheart, I know. I wish I could snap my fingers and make it all go away for you, but a mother has to let go sometime and let her babies fly from the nest."

She pushed herself to her feet and grabbed her hand to pull her up. "And while I may not be your real mom, I feel that I had more to do with your upbringing than that stupid sister of mine who made you so afraid of love. Love is always a gamble, sweetheart. You just have to place your bet and let it ride. Sometimes you win big when you stick with it long enough." She smiled at her niece as she led her into the kitchen. "But I'm still very glad that you are here, now."

"Yeah, me too. You can help with some of this cooking!" Carly complained good-naturedly, giving her a quick hug as well. "We expected you earlier. Did you get a late start out of Austin?"

"That, and Jack needed to see me in his office, so I stopped by there on my way in. So, what time does this shindig start tonight?"

"Six sharp," Helen told her, looking at her watch. "Oh, my goodness. I need to go meet Steve in town. Will you girls be alright?"

"Of course," Carly told her, as she exchanged amused looks with Nicole. "The caterer is going to be here at four-thirty and I'll make sure everything is under control." They watched Helen rush out the door, and then they sat down at the table, laughing.

"She's still a whirlwind of energy," Nicole commented.

"She never stops. And now she's fussing over me like a mother hen. I'm glad you're back, she can fuss over you for a while," Carly teased. "How long are you back for?"

"We'll see. I haven't made any job decisions yet," Nicole replied evasively. "What all do you need to do to finish up in here?"

"Are you kidding? Between Maria, the girl she brought in to help today, and Helen, everything is done. I was just putting the finishing touches on one of the desserts when you walked in, is all. I am going to go up and start getting ready, and leave the rest to the hired help!"

"Well, in that case, I'm going to go do the same." She stood up and started to walk out but turned at her friend's voice.

"By the way, Jason is supposed to be here tonight," Carly warned her friend. "He's been trying to get your cell phone number out of me."

"Thanks for the heads up. I can handle him now," Nicole smiled at her friend and went outside to get her bags out of the car. Too bad she didn't have time for a nap before this party. Something told her it was going to be a long night.

CHAPTER 18

N icole checked her reflection one last time in the mirror. She had left her hair down, brushing it out so that it fell in soft waves to her shoulders, and her makeup was flawless. She'd picked out her favorite dress, a simple black clingy number that was tight at the waist, and then flared out over her hips and fell to just below her knees. Because she was still a little self-conscious about the scars on her leg, she'd worn black stockings. She stepped into the strappy black heels, and fastened the straps. She was just putting in her earrings when a knock sounded at the bedroom door.

"Come in!" she called over her shoulder, struggling with one of the earring backs.

"Wow." Mitch whistled as he stepped into the room and caught sight of her. "Mom sent me to check on you. You about ready to join the rest of us for a drink in the living room?" She nodded, checking her hair one last time. They walked down the hallway to the living room, where Nicole greeted her uncle warmly.

"Had a man riding the fence line over by your folks' place today, said he saw a pickup there, some architect and zoning company out of Austin. The guy said he had your permission to be looking around." Steve raised his eyebrows at her. "Anything you'd like to share?"

"I asked a guy from Austin to come look around, nothing else to it." Nicole accepted the glass of wine Jack handed her as the doorbell rang.

"Was it a land developer?" he asked with a wink, causing Steve to shoot him a murderous look as he and Helen turned to leave the room to begin greeting their guests, causing Nicole to giggle. Uncle Steve hated land developers with a passion. Mitch and Carly peppered her with questions, trying to get more information about the man from Austin hanging out on her property.

"I am not ready to tell you all yet!" she laughed, bumping her cousin's arm with her elbow. "I still have a few things to think about, and once I make all of my decisions, I will let you know!" When she saw a few people walk in that she recognized as having been friends of her father's, she excused herself to go over and say hello.

Within an hour, the downstairs was full of people. Nicole knew most of them and they had all heard of her accident, so she was busy assuring them that she was fine now; no permanent damage had been done. Even though she'd been living on the ranch with Mitch and Carly all summer, she'd been pretty secluded and had kept to herself. Most of the other ranchers and their wives hadn't had a chance to see her yet until tonight. Helen kept dragging her over to the entryway to greet more old friends, but after a while, she was able to slip away and hide in a corner, talking to another area rancher that had been a good friend of her father's.

She didn't know how long he'd been at the party, but Nicole was aware of Jason as soon as he entered the room. He was standing just inside the doorway. He was looking around, and when their eyes met, she felt the jolt, almost like a bolt of lightning. She no longer paid attention to what her father's friend was saying to her. She couldn't take her eyes off of Jason. He started across the room, towards her, and she excused herself, and met him halfway.

"I need to talk to you, in private," he murmured, his eyes searching hers. "Can you break away?"

She nodded, and he took her hand, leading her through the French doors and out onto the patio, which had been converted into a dance floor for the evening. With a muttered curse, he led her down the steps and out into the garden that was Helen's pride and joy.

"God, I've missed you." He reached to take her into his arms.

"You said you wanted to talk." She reminded him, stepping back out of arms reach. Her pulse was already racing, just from the sound of his voice as well as the touch of his hand on hers. She needed to keep her hormones under control.

"I'm sorry. Yes, I do want to talk," he dropped his arms and stepped back. "I wanted to say that I was sorry for the way I acted the other morning. I have to tell you, you broadsided me with your news. I guess, after our other conversation...well, I just assumed you wouldn't give your career a second thought." When she didn't say anything, he took a step closer. "I was hurt, and angry, that we had come so far, only to be back at what I see as square one."

He reached out and took her hand, tightening his grip when she would have pulled away. "You were right, I was trying to make you give up your dreams, and if we had talked about it before, I probably would have expected you to turn the job down then, too," he admitted in a low voice.

"Where does that leave us now?" she whispered, her eyes searching his face for the answers.

"I don't know, to be honest. What did they offer you on Monday?"

"I would be department head, the position they turned me down for almost six months ago. I would only travel if there were problems on site that my team couldn't handle without me. I would be able to hire, and fire for that matter, at my own discretion. And a substantial pay increase," she told him, looking away from him. "I told them I needed to weigh all of my options, and I would give them an answer on Monday, when I meet with them again."

"What are your options?" he reached out and touched her cheek with his finger.

"I could take the job and move back to Austin, pick up where I left off before my accident," she turned back to him, meeting his intense gaze. "Or, I could stay here, start new. I have my inheritance; I could live off of that if I had to, plus my investments," she was hesitant to tell him about Jack's offer, afraid he would push her in that direction. She knew that whatever she did decide to do would affect him as well, but she just couldn't make herself confide in him, to trust him again.

"So I have until Monday morning to convince you to

stay in Waketon." He looked down at her and then bent his head and brushed her lips with his. "Will you spend Saturday with me?"

She studied him, seeing the tension, the fear and the hope in his eyes. She so wanted to dispel his doubts, but was hesitant to give in to him just yet. "If you agree to no sex," she hedged. "I need to make this decision with my head."

Smiling, he agreed, and laughing, pulled her into his arms.

"Jason..." She leaned back, a warning in her voice. "I'm serious."

"Kissing isn't sex," he whispered, holding her tight and bending his head towards her again.

"With you, it tends to lead there!" She put her hands on his chest and gave a gentle shove backwards. Chuckling, he released her, but held onto her hand. "Will you be my date for the rest of the evening?" Smiling up at him, she nodded, just as Jack wandered towards them.

"Everything okay out here?" he asked, catching and holding her gaze.

She nodded at him as Jason answered. "We're fine. I'm just trying to convince Cole to stay in Waketon."

"Good. Let me know if you need any help." Jack glanced at her again and smiled. "I have to get going. You'll let me know about Monday?" She agreed and watched him walk away.

"What's that about?" Jason asked, leading her back to the patio.

"Just stuff. You know how protective of me he gets," she answered after a brief hesitation, accepting the glass of wine he snagged off a passing waiter's tray. He reached over and cupped her cheek with his hand.

"I'm very sorry for hurting you on Saturday, Nicole. And if it is the last thing I do, I will make it up to you." He leaned over and pressed a soft kiss to her lips. "Will you dance with me?" Moving out to the dance floor, he took her in his arms. With a sigh, she dropped her head to his shoulder and closed her eyes, hearing his answering sigh as his arms tightened around her. Nicole knew what her decision was, what it had to be, and prayed that it was the right one this time.

CHAPTER 19

Nicole was sitting at the kitchen table, enjoying a second cup of coffee with Helen and Steve, when Jason arrived on Saturday.

"Good morning." He greeted them, giving Helen a kiss on the cheek and shaking Steve's hand. He stood beside Nicole's chair and leaned over to kiss her lips. "Where are Mitch and Carly?"

"They went off to Austin for the day; Carly wants to start looking at furniture for the nursery and some other baby items." Helen told him as Maria brought over another cup for him. She watched the ease with which he fit in with her family, and felt a tug at her heartstrings.

"What do you two have planned for today?" Helen asked him, looking between them.

"If she's up to it, I planned on taking her out on my boat." He raised his eyebrows at her, and Nicole nodded her head.

"That sounds like fun. Should I have Maria pack us a cooler?"

"It's all taken care of. You just need to go grab whatever it is women need for a day on a boat, and we'll head out." He smiled at her, and she found herself smiling back. She went upstairs and grabbed a couple of towels, put her swimming suit on under her shorts and t shirt, grabbed some sunscreen, and headed for the kitchen.

"Ready?" He stood up and reached out to take her beach bag from her, then grabbed her hand in his.

"We'll see you all later!" she called over her shoulder to her aunt and uncle. He led the way out to his truck, helped her up into the cab, and closed the door.

Not a lot was said between them during the ride out to the boat dock where he moored his small boat. "How often do you take her out?" she asked as she watched him stow the cooler.

He handed her a life jacket and shrugged. "Just about every weekend, depending on the weather," he answered her. "Come on, climb aboard." Holding his hand out for her to take, he helped her step down into the boat and then untied it, and gave them a push back from the dock. He moved over to the wheel and started the engine and steered them away from the dock and out to the middle of the lake.

"Where are we going?" she asked, raising her voice to be heard over the motor.

"There's a cove over there that's pretty secluded." He jerked his head to indicate the general area. "We can drop anchor and talk." Nicole nodded, and tipped her face up to the sun.

He steered them across the lake and into the small cove, where he cut the engine off and dropped the anchor overboard. Grabbing a couple of bottles of water out of the cooler, he handed one to her. He dropped down onto the bench seat in the back of the boat, and stretched his legs out in front of him, watching her. She pivoted in her seat so that they were facing each other, as she waited for him to start talking.

"Before we do anything else, I need to know one thing," he said, leaning forward and resting his elbows on his knees, holding his bottle of water with both hands.

Nicole raised her eyebrows, but didn't say anything. He took a deep breath. "I need to know how you feel about me, if you even want to try to make this work."

She turned her head to look at the trees on the banks, listening to the gentle slapping sounds the waves made against the boat. Compared to now, the years since her graduation from law school seemed empty.

Her eyes met his as she turned back to him. "I think... no, that's a cop out. I know I love you, Jason. And I do want to make this work. But..." she held up her hand as he released the breath he'd been holding and opened his mouth to say something. "But right now, I'm not sure where we stand, or what to do about it all. The second I told you that I had an opportunity to get the job that I had been cheated out of, that I had worked my entire career to get, you were ready to call it quits, not even *try* to find a solution. *If* we take another chance, start over once again, what happens the next time I get a promotion, or am asked to relocate? I can't keep doing this."

He looked down at the bottle in his hands and then back up at her. "All I can say is that I love you and I want to make it work, no matter what. You said the other day that I need to be willing to meet you halfway, and that's what I'm prepared to do. I can't lose you again."

"And the job?" she asked, her voice soft.

"If you want it, take it. If we need to move closer to Austin so that we both have to commute, we will. I'll sell the condo. I can't give up my practice here, at least not right now, but we can figure the logistics out later." He slid forward off the seat, so that he was in front of her, on his knees. He dropped the bottle of water to the floor and took her hands in his. "I love you, baby. Please, just give me another chance to prove it to you."

"You hurt me." Her eyes filled with tears and she tried to blink them away.

He let go of one of her hands and reached up to wipe the teardrops away with his thumb. He leaned in and kissed her, his mouth moving over hers in a gentle caress. "It won't happen again. I promise." He whispered, releasing a ragged sigh when he felt her arms come up and wrap around him. They stayed like that for several minutes, until Jason pushed back from her and gave her a smile.

"Feel like swimming?" He stood up and stripped off his shirt.

"No, I've never liked swimming in the lake, to be honest. I like nice, clean, chlorinated swimming pools. I'll just stay here in the boat and watch you." She pulled her own shirt off, and removed her shorts, spreading a towel out on the bow of the boat to sunbathe. Stretching out on her stomach, she closed her eyes, and between the gentle movements of the boat rocking on the waves, and the heat of the sun, she was soon asleep.

She woke up sometime later when she felt cold water

being dripped on her back. "Hey!" She rolled over and sat up, glaring at him.

"It's lunchtime." He grinned at her, holding another bottle of water out to her. "And your back is a nice shade of pink. I thought you should wake up and turn over." She took the bottle he held out to her, and moved over to make room for him as he climbed out onto the bow with her. Sitting down behind her, he leaned against the windshield and pulled her back against his chest. "Jason..."

"Shh. I just want to hold you. I missed you this week." He brushed her hair away from her neck and placed a gentle kiss in the groove of her shoulder and neck. Resting his chin on her shoulder, he wrapped his arms around her. "How was Austin?

She released a sigh and relaxed against him. "Lonely," she admitted. "I was so hurt, and angry with you. You do know that Carly offered to send Mitch and Jack after you, right?"

"I know. When Mitch called to invite me to the party the other night, he warned me I'd better watch my step around her," he rubbed his chin over her shoulder. "Are you ready to talk about your decision?"

She shook her head. "No, not until I have everything in place. There are still a few loose ends I'm waiting to tie up, and then I promise, you will be the first to know." She reached up a hand and patted his cheek. "Just be patient, little boy!" she teased with a soft laugh.

"Not one of my virtues," he grumbled, turning his head and kissing her palm. "You ready to head back to the dock? I planned to serve you lunch at my condo." She agreed and they settled back into the boat. He pulled in the anchor and steered the boat back across the lake to the dock. They loaded their things into his truck and he drove them over to his apartment.

"Whoa!" she stepped into the condo and stopped short, looking around in amazement. "What's all this?" Stunned, she turned around to look at Jason. Every surface in the apartment held a bouquet of flowers, in every color imaginable.

He grinned at her as he stepped around her, grabbing her hand and leading her to the kitchen. Indicating the white florist's box on the counter, he stepped back as she opened it. She gasped as she unwrapped the two dozen red roses wrapped in green tissue paper.

"Oh, Jason," she sighed, her eyes welling with tears.

"A long time ago, you told me how much you loved flowers and that you'd never gotten any from a boy. At the time, my parents had me living on a pretty tight budget, and I wasn't about to explain why I needed money to buy flowers. I'm sure the local florist shops will be out of flowers for the next few days. I was only going to get the roses but I needed to show you how sorry I am for the way we left things last Saturday," he stepped around her. "I needed to replace that memory with a much nicer one."

He took her hand and led her into the living room, where the furniture had been pushed back and a picnic lunch had been laid out on the floor. "If it wasn't over eighty degrees outside, I'd turn the gas fireplace on and really romance you." After helping her get situated on the blanket, he moved over to the iPod and speaker and turned on some soft music.

"How did you get all of this done?" she asked him, looking around in amazement.

"Carly and Mitch didn't go to Austin today. Mitch agreed to come over and move the furniture, and Carly went to get the food for me, and let the florists in when they arrived. Helen can't keep a secret, so they told her they were headed to Austin," he explained, opening a bottle of wine and filling the two glasses in the picnic basket. He handed one to her, and then stretched out on the blanket next to her, propping himself up on an elbow.

"To us," he whispered, clinking his glass against hers. She took a sip of the wine, and nodded in approval.

"What else do you have in there?" she asked, tipping her head towards the basket.

"All of your picnic essentials. There's fried chicken, still warm, potato salad, fruit, and chocolate dessert." He sat up and began pulling the items out of the basket. "Are you hungry?"

"Mmm-hmm." She took the plate he handed her and filled it up. The music from the speakers filled the silence between as they ate. Once they'd stuffed themselves, Jason moved the picnic basket out of the way and reached to pull her down on the blanket, stretching out beside her. She was on her back, and he leaned over her. He reached up with one hand and smoothed the hair back away from her face, leaning down to kiss her. She reached up and wrapped her arms around his neck, allowing him to deepen the kiss. His hand traced a path from her throat to her stomach, and then he pushed her shirt up and groaned. "I forgot you had your bathing suit on."

She laughed and pushed him away. "We agreed that

there would be no sex, remember?" she pushed herself to her feet and moved over to the window.

"Copping a feel and making out do not constitute sex," he defended himself, standing up. "But if it makes you uncomfortable..."

"It's not that I'm uncomfortable, Jason," she turned back to face him. "I don't need to cloud my judgment any more than I already have. You have this ability to make me throw my good sense and reason out the window, and let my hormones take over. *If* I decide to stay in Waketon, it has to be because I want to for me, not because you're good in bed."

"Ouch," Jason playfully rubbed a hand over his heart and stepped closer to her. "Okay, I won't try to coerce you back into my bed until after your decision is made. How's that?" He held his hand out to her, and after a brief hesitation, she reached out and put her hand in his. Pulling her in closer, he wrapped his arms around her, her head on his chest.

"I suppose, then, I should take you home before I get carried away. Because when I am with you, all I can think about is getting you naked and in between the sheets," he whispered in her ear, causing her to blush. He chuckled, and plucked one of the roses out of its vase and handed to her. "Here, take this home with you and think of me tonight when you are all alone in your bed."

"So, what are your plans for tomorrow?" he asked as they drove back to the ranch.

"I'm going to drive back up to Austin. I have a few appointments to keep, and I owe Robert my decision." she told him, glancing down at their joined hands, waiting to see if he drew away. He rubbed his thumb over her knuckles.

"I'm on call again tomorrow, but will you call me to let me know you got to Austin?" He asked, keeping his eyes on the road. "And let me know when you'll be back?"

"Of course." She gave his hand a gentle squeeze. "I'm not trying to play mind games or be a tease. I just need..."

"It's okay, Nicole. I get it. I may not like it, but I do get it." He pulled the truck up in front of the ranch house and climbed out, coming around to hold the door and help her out. "But know this right now: I am not going to give up, and I am not going to let you give up. Not this time." He pulled her up against him and gave her a hard kiss, leaving them both breathing heavy when he broke away. "I'll talk to you later." He walked around the truck, climbed back in, and drove off in a cloud of dust. She climbed the porch steps, glanced at Mitch with a look that dared him to make even one comment, and headed inside and to her room.

She laid the rose she had brought home with her down on the dresser before sitting down in the chair next to the window, her phone in her hand. This had become her favorite spot since coming back to the ranch. Since this bedroom was located in the back of the house, it was quiet, allowing her to think in peace. She stared out at the rolling hills, the mountains in the distance. Her father had loved this land, loved working the ranch. He'd been so proud of her, encouraging her to do well in school so she could get into the University of Texas. And he was so different from her mother.

She glanced down at her phone and hit the button to dial Jack's number.

"Hey. I thought you had a date with Jason today," he answered on the second ring.

"I did. He just dropped me off a little while ago," she cleared her throat. "I need a favor."

"Is it going to cost me any friends?"

"Just me, if you don't help me," she threatened. "I want to go through my stuff."

"It's in the garage there. All the boxes should be labeled."

"No, I mean the stuff from before," she clarified, "from my parents' house."

"Oh." Jack was quiet. "Why now?"

"Jason said something last week that's been bothering me, made me start thinking about everything." She took a deep breath. "Mom didn't leave a note, she always left a note. And who called Dad? No one ever admitted to being the one to call him."

"Are you saying you don't think he did it?"

"I'm saying I have questions that I'm ready to get answers to. I need the closure, Jack. Whether this thing with Jason goes anywhere or not, I need to move past this."

He was silent for so long, she was afraid the phone had dropped the call. "OK, I can come over in the morning. You know Mitch and Carly will want to help."

"They're going over to Carly's mom's house, spending the whole day."

"I'll be there by ten o'clock. What about Austin?" Jack asked.

"I'll drive up tomorrow night, or Monday morning," Nicole closed her eyes. "I owe you one, Jack."

"I'll come up with something good. See you in the

morning," he hung up and Nicole slipped her phone into her pocket, staring out her window.

She was ready to face her past and move onto her future. Her decision about the job was made, she knew what she was going to do, and she just had a few more details to work out. The next few days were going to be long.

CHAPTER 20

N icole was waiting on the porch when jack arrived the next morning. Her foot tapped out an impatient beat and she held her arm up, pointing at her watch. He shook his head but gave her a grin as he climbed the steps.

"Where are Ma and Pop?" he asked, using the names he'd given Helen and Steve a long time ago. He reached for her coffee and she held it out of reach.

"Do it and die." She narrowed her eyes at him, "Go get your own. Helen and Steve are in the kitchen, where the coffee is."

Laughing, Jack headed inside. Nicole shook her head and sighed, leaning against the porch railing. Knowing Jack, he'd be in there for a couple of minutes, at least. She just wanted to get this done and over with. The possibility that her mother *had* left a note was driving her crazy. If there was a note, would it answer any questions or just add to them? And did she even want to know what her mother had been thinking?

Jack came back out a few minutes later with a thermos of coffee. "Here, Ma fixed this for us," he handed the thermos over to her. "Walk or drive down to the storage barn?" he jerked his thumb at one of the off-road vehicles.

"I can handle the walk if you can," she glanced at the scar showing below his basketball shorts.

"Want to race?"

"I said I could *walk* it. I'm not running in this heat." Nicole frowned as she pulled her hair up into a ponytail. "Let's go," she headed down the steps.

Chuckling, he caught up with her and slung his arm around her shoulders. "So, how are things going with Jason?"

"He took me out on his boat yesterday and we've talked." She looked at him from the corner of her eye. "I've fallen in love with him again, Jack."

"Yeah, I figured as much." She felt his arm tighten around her. "Are we celebrating this fact, or do I need to help you move somewhere out of state?"

"I'm not running away this time."

"Good to know," he grinned at her. "I'd hate to have to kick your ass."

"Better be nice, or I'll start looking for a girlfriend for you," she elbowed him in the ribs, but the smile died as they stepped up to the storage garage. It used to have equipment in it, but Steve had built a bigger structure farther away from the house to keep noise levels down.

"You sure about this?" Jack kept his eyes on her as she bit her lip and took a couple of deep breaths. She nodded, pulling the key out of her pocket.

"I'm sure. I have no idea what we'll find, or even what

the hell we're looking for, but I want to do this." She unlocked the barn style doors and together, they pushed them open.

"Ma needs to have a garage sale," he muttered, sneezing at all the dust that was disturbed by the slight breeze. Frowning, he looked around the large structure. Every piece of furniture that had ever been replaced in the house was in here. Along with old toys, textbooks from their college days, and anything else none of them wanted in the house, but didn't want to get rid of.

"Don't even suggest it to her. She'll rope all of us into dragging this stuff out of here and going through it!" Nicole flipped a couple of switches, turning lights on throughout the building.

"Ok, where do we start?" Jack opened the thermos and refilled their cups.

"Aunt Helen said most of the stuff from my parents is in that back corner," she pointed to one of the corners of the building and they made their way to it. "Thank God she's made sure there are pathways between things."

"At least she knows where she's put stuff," Jack grumbled, taking in all the boxes. "How do you want to do this?"

"Just start going through the boxes, I guess," she grimaced as she looked at the number of containers stacked around them. Grabbing one of the boxes, she pulled out a box cutter, exposing the blade. She sliced through the tape and opened the one closest to her. "These are just books," she closed it and started to shift it out of her way.

"Hold up," Jack laid his hand on her arm, stopping her. "Think this through with me. Your mom is trying to leave; she's in a hurry to get packed and out the door. We're not sure who called your dad, right?" Nicole nodded her head in answer and he continued. "So, we're not sure she even knows that her time is limited."

"I didn't notice anything out of the ordinary that day when I got back from the lake," she shared, watching as he dusted off an old chair and sat down. "I mean, nothing was out of place, and until the police said she was trying to leave, I didn't notice anything missing. Even then, it was just the suitcase and some clothes. Other than that, everything was like it should be. Except for the lack of a note. Mom was a stickler for leaving notes."

"What if she just didn't leave it where she would on a normal day, because she didn't want your father to find it?"

Nicole looked around at the boxes. "*If* that's what happened she would have left a note in my room. But I was in my room when I got home that day; there wasn't a note."

"Well, not out where you saw it, anyway," he agreed, standing back up. "So, let's find the stuff from your room."

"Most of my stuff came with me when I moved over. It was just the furniture that got moved out here," Nicole stopped him. She turned back to study the area, considering the options that he'd just laid out. "My desk!"

"What?"

"I didn't bring my desk to the house with me. My room here already had one and I didn't see the point in moving it out to bring in mine." Her eyes swept around the area, looking for it. "I had Aunt Helen give away most of the furniture in the house, but that desk was one of the few things I wanted to keep."

"Is that it?" he pointed to the far wall, where a desk was pushed into the corner with boxes were piled around it.

Nicole nodded and they made their way to it. "Wouldn't the desk have been emptied out before it was moved over here?"

"Yes, but it had a secret bottom in the top drawer. I found it by accident. When she was in one of her fun moods, Mom would hide little trinkets in there for me," she stood with her hands on her hips looking at the desk. "She wasn't always such a bitch."

Jack stepped up beside her, mimicking her stance. "I know. I remember a couple of times, when we were much younger, she'd bake cookies with us," he turned his head to look at her. "It's hard to remember those times when she was a shrew most of the time."

Nicole nodded and indicated the boxes on the floor in front of the desk. "We need to get this stack out of the way so we can get into that drawer," she tapped the bottom one with her foot.

"Alright, I think we can just slide them across the floor," Jack told her, testing the weight of the stack. "They're not too heavy." Together, they knelt on the floor and shoved them out of their way. Nicole stood up and moved over to the desk, staring at it, her hand clenching and unclenching at her side.

"Nicole...we don't have to do this," Jack reminded her, and even though his voice was low, in the quiet of the old barn, it seemed to bellow.

"Yeah, Jack, I do," she reached out and pulled the drawer open, running her fingers along the edge. There was a soft 'snick' as the mechanism released and the false bottom sprung open. "There's something here," Nicole looked over at Jack, her eyes wide with surprise.

The envelope she withdrew from the drawer had started to turn yellow with age, but the writing on the outside was still legible. Turning the envelope over in her hands, she stared at the writing. "It's from Mom," she whispered.

"Do you want to open it here, or take it up to the house?" Jack stepped up beside her and placed a hand on her shoulder.

"The house," she answered without hesitation. "I'm not sure what I want to do with it now." Her eyes roamed around the old barn. "I'm a little afraid to read it, to be honest."

"I know, kiddo." Jack squeezed her shoulder and then indicated the doors behind them. "Do you want to head back up there, or go through some of these boxes? What's in them, anyway?"

"Books, for the most part. A few of the boxes have Dad's rodeo stuff and Mom's knick-knacks," she looked around. "Anything I didn't want right away, or that Aunt Helen thought I might want in the future."

"We could go through a few of them," he offered.

"Not today. I think I just want to go back up to the house," she shook her head. "You're welcome to stay and go through them."

Jack looked at the stacks of boxes. "No, I'll walk back up with you. I wanted to talk to Pop about some stuff." They both moved towards the doors. Making sure the lights were off, Jack closed and locked the doors.

"How soon are you going to head to Austin?" he asked as they turned to walk back up to the house.

"I was thinking later this afternoon. Jason is on call so

I'm just going to hang around, get a few things figured out," she tapped the envelope with a finger.

"You know how to find me if you need me," he nudged her arm with his elbow as they climbed the steps to the front porch.

"That I do," she agreed with a grateful smile. "I'm going to go stare at this thing for a while."

Shutting her bedroom behind her, Nicole set the envelope down on her dresser and then sat on the end of her bed. She closed her eyes and took a deep breath. *What am I so afraid of? Maybe I'll get the answers I've wanted, once and for all.* She stood back up and snatched the envelope off the bed, walking over to her window and staring out at the ranch. Folding the envelope in half, she shoved it into her back pocket and turned to the closet, grabbing her riding boots. She knew where she needed to go to read this.

Forty-five minutes later, she tethered her horse to a bush near the pond and climbed up onto one of the rocks, its surface warm from the sun. Closing her eyes, she tilted her head back, absorbing the sun, enjoying the quiet of nature for a moment. With a sigh, she pulled the envelope out of her back pocket and tore it open, pulling out two sheets of paper. It was dated the day before her parents had died. With one last deep breath to calm her nerves, she started reading.

Dear Nicole,

By the time you read this, I will be gone. I'm planning to hide it in your desk, so who knows how long it will be before you find it. It will be up to you what you want to do with it... read it, burn it, show it to everyone. But it's time for you to know the truth.

"Hell if that line didn't just say it all," Nicole muttered out loud, before returning to the words on the page.

First, let's get this out in the open. I know I was a lousy mother. You deserved so much more from me, but I want you to know it was never you. It was me. Sounds like a cop-out, doesn't it? But it's true, and I hope you've realized that.

I know Helen has told you about our childhood. It wasn't easy. She was lucky to find your Uncle Steve. He's the total opposite of the asshole who fathered us. I know everyone thinks I'm jealous of the money they have. But it wasn't the money, it was the love between them I was jealous of. Steve and Helen took me in, gave me a home.

Don't get me wrong. I did—and part of me always will— love your dad. He saved me, and you, but I wasn't 'in love' with him. I had nothing against him being a rancher or the foreman for Steve. He worked hard, made an honest living, provided everything we needed. I chose to make it about the money because to admit it was anything else after everything he did for me would have destroyed him. And you. I never wanted that.

But as I said, it's time for you to know the truth. Someday, I hope to come back and talk to you. But I'm a coward.

The truth, my beautiful child, is that the man you call your dad, is not your biological father. I was already pregnant when I married him. He knew I was pregnant and he wanted to give you a name.

And as I said, I was a coward. I saw what this town did

to Jack's mother, although her situation was a little different, but small town life is not kind to an unwed mother. I promised your dad I would never tell you the truth. But I can't be true to myself, living a lie.

Your dad found me crying down by the creek the day I found out I was pregnant with you. I told him the whole sorry tale. Your typical 'stupid teenager who had sex without protection tale,' I'm afraid. I'd gone to Austin for a weekend with some friends, talked our way into some of the bars on Sixth Street, and met a guy. He was a young soldier, stationed up at Fort Hood. We spent twenty-four hours together. That was it. But it gave me you.

I knew I couldn't have an abortion, but I also knew I couldn't make it on my own. And there's no way I would have been able to hold my head up in this town. And I didn't want you labeled a 'bastard' or to have to answer for my sins.

"Well, I did anyway," Nicole remarked, the bitterness of it all leaving an unpleasant feeling in her gut. She forced herself to keep reading.

I'm sorry, honey. I know how much you love your dad, and I don't want that to change. He is the man who has been there from day one for you. And he loves you. He always wanted a child, but he couldn't have any of his own.

So he offered to marry me, and raise you as his own. He promised to keep my secret. I didn't know how to get in touch with the man who got me pregnant. His unit was at Fort Hood for training and then they were going to be deployed. I didn't have an address or a phone number. So he never knew you even existed.

I've lived this lie for almost sixteen years now. And a little piece of me has died every day. All my comments about giving life up if you marry the wrong man or have children, well, that was my fear and cowardice talking. If you find the right man, he makes you complete. Your father tried to be that man for me, but although I loved him for what he'd done for us, it was never the passionate love either of us deserved.

And now, I think I have found that love. I'm too afraid to ask for a divorce. Your dad has talked me out of it before. If I leave, he can file for it on the grounds of abandonment. I do believe you'll both be better off without me.

Someday, I hope to come back, let you confront me, tell me you hate me, whatever you need to do. And I will stand there and let you. But know this, I never hated you. I was hard on you, maybe too hard, but I didn't want you to ever make the mistakes I did. I wanted you to be able to go to college, become a lawyer like you've been talking about. I made a lot of mistakes, sweet girl, but you were not one of them. I took my regrets out on you. I realize that now. And I'm sorry. So very sorry. I hope someday you can forgive me.

Love,

Mom

Nicole dropped the letter to her lap and allowed the tears to fall. Tears for her mother, who hadn't felt like she had any control over her life, tears for her father, who'd given them his name and taken care of them, and tears for all the lost years and the anger.

It didn't answer the question as to why her father had killed her mother. She may never know that answer. But at least now, she had some understanding about her mother. It may not be much, but it was more than she'd had to start.

. . .

NICOLE WAITED until early Monday morning to make the drive to Austin. After the emotional upheaval over the past few days, she needed the time to get it together. She'd talked to her aunt after getting back to the house, and had called Jason to tell him her plans had changed, but she'd begged everyone to let her process the information first. She wasn't ready to talk about it. With time before her meeting with Robert, she drove over to the office of the land surveyor she'd hired the week before, and picked up his report. The architect had emailed her his report earlier in the week, and it was in her attaché case as well.

Parking in downtown Austin was a rare commodity, so she pulled into one of the public garages and walked to the small coffee shop near the law office. She slid the reports out of the file and read through them. She'd have time later to study them in depth, but at that moment she just wanted to see what the bottom line was. With a small smile, she slid the papers back into her attaché case and looked out of the coffee shops windows at the city around her. Her decision firm, she stood up and walked across the street to her old office building and her meeting with Robert. Only one of them was going to leave this meeting happy.

FOUR HOURS LATER, she was back in Waketon, parked in front of Jason's condo. She knew he planned to take today off from his office after having been on call the day before, or at least that is what he had told her when she'd called him the night before. Wetting her lips, she rang the door-bell, and waited for him to answer.

"Nicole! I wasn't expecting to hear from you until

tonight. Come on in!" He was dressed in jeans and a t shirt, unshaven and disheveled. He held the door open for her. He followed behind as she walked into the living room, watching as she took in the all of the flowers that were still there, a smile on her lips.

"I take it you made your decision," he walked over to stand beside her, shoving his hands into the back pocket of his jeans, the tension radiating from him.

"I've been rehearsing my speech the entire way from Austin to Waketon." Nicole admitted, her eyes meeting his.

I'd hate to be playing poker with her; her face is giving nothing away at all. Jason thought as he tried to read her body language. "And?" he prompted when she didn't say anything.

She walked over to the windows, looking out over the lake. "Ten years ago, I chose a job and career over you, and ignored what I felt, because I was scared. It had been drilled into me since birth to never let a man control me. I was young, and naïve, and afraid that I'd end up like my mother if I gave in to what my heart was telling me to do. I had spent fifteen years watching her and my father make each other miserable and I never understood why. Now, I have a better understanding but I don't think I'll ever understand why my father did what he did." Turning to face Jason, she smiled.

"I've always let the past dictate how my future was going to be played out. When we met, I let you in and you got to me and I panicked and forced myself to walk away. And I never thought I'd get a second chance, until about three months ago when I almost killed myself in a car accident, and had to come back to Waketon. And even then you were so indifferent to me at first; I thought I had blown it."

"Cole, please, you're killing me here. Tell me what you decided," he groaned. He stood ramrod straight and she could see the tension in his face. Pushing away from the window sill, she walked over to stand in front of him. As she reached up and laid her palm against his cheek, the stubble from his five o'clock shadow scratching her tender skin, she smiled at him, allowing all the love she'd ever felt to shine through.

"I told Robert that I wasn't interested in returning to work for him. It's time I returned home, to Waketon. I want to start a new life, build a house, maybe buy a few horses, and get a dog." She looked up at him, seeing the hope start to flare in his eyes. "Maybe even a husband..."

"I think I know someone who might like to apply for that position." He murmured, his hands coming up to rest on her waist. "But are you sure?"

Without hesitation, she nodded, her hand caressing his face. "All last week, and again today, while I was in Austin, I kept watching everyone hurrying around, and I just couldn't picture myself there anymore. And talking with Robert, well, even though they did offer me the job, I was their second choice. They didn't listen to me six months ago when I tried to tell them what a mistake they were making. That grates, you know?" He pulled her to him and wrapped his arms around her, tight. She laid her head on his chest, feeling the rapid heartbeat against her cheek. "I tried to picture myself moving back to Austin, picking up the pieces of my life there, and not having you there with me, and I couldn't do it. I couldn't picture a life without you anymore. Which leads me to the most important reason: I love you."

He threaded his fingers in her hair and pulled her head back so he could claim her lips.

"Are you going to be happy, not working, though?" he asked her, leading her over to the couch and pulling her down on his lap.

"I didn't say I wouldn't be working." She pointed out. "I said I wouldn't be working for Robert." She traced a finger around his lips, causing them to twitch. "Jack talked to me last week and offered me a job. Which reminds me, I need to call him and give him my decision."

"He's been talking about hiring a second person for the business. I'm glad he offered it to you." Capturing her wandering hands in his, he kissed her palms. "Tell me again that you're staying." He leaned in for another kiss.

"I'm staying, and rebuilding my life, here in Waketon... with you," she whispered against his mouth. She pushed him back before he could get too carried away. "We need to talk about what we're going to do next." It was her turn to grab his wrists to keep his hands from undressing her.

"My plan was to get you naked and into bed."

"Jason..." She laughed and pushed herself off his lap. "Be serious."

"I am. I am serious that I want you naked, in my bed." He reached out to try and grab her but she moved out of reach. He stood up and moved over to stand in front of her, and grabbed her hands. "I told you that first night, I plan on marrying you. That hasn't changed. And you just talked about all kinds of plans you have. What else is there?" He tugged on her hands, pulling her against him. "We can iron out specifics later," he whispered, trailing kisses along her jawline.

With a moan, she gave in and wrapped her arms around his broad shoulders. Feeling her surrender, he bent and swung her up in his arms and carried her off to the bedroom.

CHAPTER 21

Nicole woke up, alone in jason's bed. The room was dark so she assumed it had to be several hours since he'd carried her to his room. She rolled over to look at the clock and was surprised to see that it was after ten o'clock. Groaning, she pushed herself into a sitting position, and, wrapping the sheet around her, started to climb out of bed.

"Where do you think you're going?" Jason asked from behind her. She looked over her shoulder and saw him carrying a tray with food and drinks on it through the doorway. Setting the tray down on the dresser by the bed, he turned to face her, hands on his hips. His jeans low rode on his hips, the top button undone, and no shirt. The sight of his flat abdomen and the thick muscles of his chest had her struggling to remember to breathe.

"I need to get going. I'm sure Helen and Carly are worried about me by now." Nicole tried to move around him, but Jason stopped her.

"I called and talked to Mitch. I told him not to expect

you home tonight." He gave her a gentle push back onto the bed, and leaned over her, placing his hands on either side of her. "I put together a snack for you." He indicated the tray he'd brought in with a nod of his head. "Are you hungry?"

"A little," she nodded.

He smiled down at her, kissed the tip of her nose, and then pushed away from the bed to bring the tray over to her, while she sat up.

"Will this tide you over?" He placed the tray across her lap, and she studied the tray of cheese, crackers and fruit he'd brought her.

"This will be fine," she assured him, nibbling on a piece of cheese.

"Work on that, then. I'll be back." He winked at her and headed back out to the living room. She ate the snack he'd brought her and pushed the tray aside and, trying to keep the sheet wrapped around her, she climbed out of the bed and stepped into the bathroom. Feeling exposed, she grabbed his robe off the bathroom door. After wrapping it around herself as tight as she could without cutting off the ability to breathe, she opened the door, her steps faltering at the sight of him sitting on the end of the bed. Beside him was a single red rose.

He looked up and gave her his heart stopping smiles, and opened his arms. Without hesitation, she walked over to him and allowed him to settle her on his lap.

"Feeling better?" he asked.

She nodded with a smile. His arms wrapped around her and he bent his head to kiss her before bending her backwards to lay her on the bed, stretching out next to her, propping himself up on one elbow. Tucking her hair back away from her face, he cupped her cheek with his hand, stroking her cheek with his fingertips, his thumb feeling the accelerating pulse in her throat. Leaning down, he placed a soft kiss on that pulse, and then a series of kisses down her neck, to where the robe had fallen away from her shoulder.

With a groan, he pushed himself up, and reached for the rose he'd laid down at the foot of the bed, and handed it to her. "I've loved you for over ten years, Cole. Even when we were separated, there was a part of me that always prayed you would come back to me." He stretched out on the bed beside her and pulled her across his chest, his hands caressing her back through the bulk of the cotton robe. "I want to spend the rest of my life proving to you how much I love you." He captured her left hand and slid a ring onto her ring finger. "Nicole Winters, will you marry me?"

Tears filling her eyes, she stared down at the ring and nodded.

"Is that a yes?"

"Oh, yes!" The tears fell, and Jason reached up, wiping them away with his fingertips.

"Don't cry, sweetheart. God, I love you. You are my whole world, babe," he kissed her again, nipping at her lower lip and then soothing the sting away with his tongue.

"I love you, too. So much," she told him on a moan, her head tilting back, exposing her neck to his wandering lips.

"Can you take me again?" he whispered, bending his head and kissing the exposed skin of one breast, where the robe gaped open.

She reached down and undid the zipper of his jeans, freeing him. "What do you think?"

He grinned at her and rolled them over before untying the belt holding the robe together. Pushing it off her shoulders, he leaned over and tongued one of her nipples, smiling against her breast when it hardened. Not able to stop the moan from escaping, she arched her back, her fingernails digging into his shoulders. He pulled the robe off of her as she helped him out of his jeans. When he reached for her, she pushed him back on the bed and leaned over him.

"It's my turn," she whispered. "I want to torment you, like you've been tormenting me."

His eyes blazed and his fingers flexed against her shoulders. "Torment, huh? What do you have in mind?"

Flicking her tongue at one of his nipples, her hand stroked down the hard muscles of his abdomen, and lower to his groin, eliciting a groan from him. Her mouth and hands drove him crazy, until he couldn't take it anymore, and he was begging her to end his torment. She laughed and straddled his hips, taking him deep inside, sighing as he stretched her. He grabbed her hips and guided her, taking them both over the edge, as she collapsed onto his chest.

"Wow! Where the hell did you learn to do that?" he groaned out, sometime later, with her still sprawled across his chest.

"It just comes natural when I'm with you," she murmured.

"Not going to complain about that," he kissed the top of her head as his hand rubbed up and down her back, causing her to arch against him, like a cat. He grinned and continued to rub her back, liking her movements against him. She shivered and his arms wrapped around her, pulling her against his warmth. "You okay?" he murmured.

"Never better," she assured him as she shifted off his chest but kept her head on his shoulder.

He let her go, but kept one arm around her, needing that connection with her. Holding her left hand out in front of them, she admired the ring he'd placed there. It was a simple princess cut diamond in a traditional setting. The stone caught and flashed in the soft light from the bedside table.

"If you don't like it, we can go shopping, pick out a different one," he offered, reaching out his own finger to touch the ring.

"This one is perfect. When did you buy it?" Turning onto her side, she propped herself up on an elbow.

"After our first night together, I snuck out for a bit the afternoon I was on call." He reached up and tucked her hair behind her ear, out of their faces. "I was going to give it to you that Saturday morning, over breakfast, but you know how that ended..." he grimaced. Cupping the back of her head, he guided her mouth down to his. "How long are you going to make me wait?"

"Good God, aren't you tired?" She pushed herself back, her eyes wide.

Laughing, he wrapped his arms around her and pulled her back down to his chest. "Tired and empty for the moment; I meant, how long are you going to make me wait until you marry me?"

"I guess that depends on where you want to live. A house can take three to six months to build, don't forget," she pointed out, her fingers playing with his defined pec muscles.

"We could live here until the house is built, unless you have something against this place." His hand was sending shivers of delight down her spine. "So, how long?" he prompted.

"December?" she suggested.

"December?! That's four months away. I was thinking next month," he countered.

"Next month? As in September? That's so...sudden."

"Given our history, it's not that sudden. And it's not like the guest list has to be huge. My only family is my half-sister and she's on tour in Europe right now with that band. I'm not sure she could take the time to come in for it. We don't have to have a large wedding, do we?" he reached out to caress her cheek with his fingertips. "But I guess I can wait a few months, if you have your heart set on a December wedding."

"No, it's not that..." she pushed away from him and left the bed, grabbing the robe off the floor and once again wrapping it around herself, needing the flimsy security it offered her. Still tying the belt, she turned around and faced Jason, who was still lying in bed, his arms now tucked behind his head. "It's so sudden *for me*. We've only been back together a few weeks, and now we're engaged, and you want to get married next month. I just need some time." Her eyes were pleading with him, begging him to under-stand. She didn't know what she'd do if he forced the issue, or walked away again.

He dragged himself up and off the bed and moved over to stand in front of her. Gripping her shoulders, he pressed a kiss to her forehead. "You can have all the time you need. You need to slow it down? Fine, we'll slow it down." He told her in an even voice. "I promised you I wouldn't push you, or rush you, and I'm sorry if you feel if I've done just that. I lost you once, I don't want to go through that again. Please, just don't panic on me, okay?"

She swallowed hard and nodded, allowing him to pull her up against his chest. Wrapped up in his arms, the fears and insecurities started to fade away. Laying her head on his chest, she put her trust in this man that she loved. But she couldn't shake the feeling that the other shoe was just waiting to drop.

CHAPTER 22

Nicole woke up the next morning, alone in Jason's bed, still wrapped in his robe. Stretching, she forced herself to get out of his bed and took a quick shower. She'd been surprised to see find her overnight back sitting on her counter. Reminding herself to thank him for going out to her car to get it, she dressed in her clean jeans and shirt before towel drying her hair. She straightened the sheets on the bed, and then, taking a deep breath, walked out of the bedroom. Smelling fresh coffee, she headed for the kitchen, and found Jason leaning against the counter, concentrating on whatever was on his phone's screen.

"Hi," she whispered.

"Hi." He set the phone aside and held out his hand. A little hesitant, she allowed him to draw her into his embrace. "How do you feel this morning?" He held her close and she relaxed against him.

"Like this is all a dream." She sighed before stepping back. "I'm sure you need to get to the office."

"Yeah, I have a full schedule today, and a few surgeries scheduled for tomorrow that I need to prep for. With any luck, I'll be out of there by five, if my patients are on time. At least I won't be on call again until the middle of next week." He picked his cell phone back up and slipped it into his bag. "What's on your agenda?"

"I need to go back to the ranch, and I need to talk to Jack; iron out the specifics of his offer." She turned towards him after pouring herself a cup of coffee, taking a moment to look him over. He was dressed in khaki's and a light blue polo shirt, which brought out the blue of his eyes.

"Here," he said before taking a key from his pocket and holding it out to her. "It's to the condo," he explained, noticing her eyebrow rising at the sight of it. "You can come and go as you want. You could even move some of your stuff over from the ranch so you don't have to pack a bag every night."

"Jason..." She stared down at it.

"It's just to make things a little easier, Nicole. Use it or don't. It's your decision. Right now, I have to get to work." Grabbing the shoulder strap of his bag, he slung it over his shoulder. "Will I see you tonight?" He turned to look at her from the doorway, his impatience with her hesitations evident in his expression.

"I'll be here," she promised, her eyes begging for time and understanding.

He muttered something under his breath and then crossed the kitchen to stand in front of her.

"You have to meet me halfway, babe. I can't do it all on my own," he reminded her, leaning over and giving her a hard kiss. "I'll see you tonight." He turned and headed out the door, leaving her alone in the kitchen.

Nicole released a ragged breath and turned to the sink, dumping her coffee down the drain. Her stomach was churning enough right now, she didn't need to add any more acid to it, she decided. She made sure the coffee pot was turned off before grabbing her own bag out of the bedroom, wanting to escape to the simplicity of the ranch.

"Hey, you, it's about time you came home," Carly greeted her from the porch when she stepped out of her car. Nicole climbed the steps and joined her friend on the porch swing.

"Sorry, Jason said he'd talked to Mitch last night..."

"He did, but he didn't tell him anything, other than you were at his place and for us not to expect you home," Carly agreed, reaching over and tapping the ring on her friend's finger. "It looks like he left out a few tiny details," she teased.

Nicole smiled, and held her hand out. "Jason proposed, and I accepted."

Carly ooh'd and ahh'd over the ring for a few seconds and then examined her friend's face. "For someone who is grabbing hold of the brass ring, you don't look too excited," she remarked.

Nicole leaned her head back and closed her eyes, letting out a ragged sigh. "One minute everything seems so clear, and the next, I'm scared to death and unsure of every-thing." She sat back up and met Carly's concerned gaze. "Were you like this with Mitch?"

KELLI HENEGHAN

"To some extent, I'd say yes." Carly set the swing back into motion with a push of her foot. "But I'd been in love with Mitch since we were kids." she reminded her. Carly looked at her out of the corner of her eye. "I'm assuming you turned down that job in Austin?"

"I did. Jack made me an offer, and I'm going to take the job with him. Speaking of which..." Nicole glanced at her watch. "I need to call Jack and tell him, too."

"He can wait another few minutes then," Carly stopped her from getting up off the swing with a hand on her arm. "Come on, Nicole. Tell me what's wrong. You do love Jason, don't you?"

Nicole sat back and looked out over the land. "I do, and he says he loves me," she agreed. "It's just...It's so fast, you know?"

"You've known each other for ten years," Carly pointed out, echoing Jason's words to her.

"But we haven't been around each other for all of those years! And I assumed he hated me after the way I walked away without discussing it with him."

"But you've discussed it now, right? And you know he's not just giving lip service to the words. Anybody with eyes can tell that man does love you, Nicole."

"Yes, we've talked about what happened between us before. And I know he loves me, but..."

"But what?" Carly prompted.

"What happens if..."

"What happens happens, Nicole." Carly cut her off. "Look, you had a rough break with your mom, and you've let it rule your life since...well, forever. You're a big girl now, and the choice is yours alone to make. You can reach out, grab on, and take the ride of a lifetime, or you can continue to sit on the sidelines and wonder about what could have been. At least if you take the chance, you'll never look back and wonder." Carly stopped the swing and stood up. "And talk to Jason. You'd be surprised at the obstacles love can help you overcome, if you do it together." She gave her friend a soft smile with that piece of advice before turning to head back inside.

Nicole sat on the porch thinking about what Carly had said, what everyone had been saying for the past few weeks. Her heart was telling her—begging her—to listen to them. The letter from her mother that she and Jack had found had explained so much, but raised so many other questions. Questions she knew she would never get an answer to, not after this much time. Who had her mother met and been attracted to and why had her father killed her and then taken his own life? And who had called her father that day, telling him her mother was leaving? She stared out at the ranch, for the first time feeling more anger towards her father than she did towards her mother. Before reading that letter, it had been easy to hate her mother, to be glad she was gone. But now, she had it in writing that her mother *had* loved her and cared about her.

So what do I do about me and Jason? she asked herself as she looked out at the land. She loved him and he loved her, she didn't doubt that, not anymore. Would moving in with him change anything? Their relationship was so new, at least, the rediscovery of their true feelings was new. She could never get back all those years they'd lost, but they could carve out their future together. Holding out her hand, she looked down at the diamond ring on her finger, as her thumb rubbed across the band. "No regrets, Mom," she whispered as she stood up.

It didn't take her long to pack a couple of bags. She'd be able to drive back over anytime, if she forgot anything. She headed out to the living room to find Helen and Carly.

"Hi, honey. Come join us. We're just looking at all the furniture we need to order for a nursery." Helen patted the seat beside her.

"No, thanks. I'm going to go see Jack, let him know he has a new partner." She smiled at them.

"You're moving in with him?" Helen asked nodding towards the suitcase beside her and the duffel bag she had slung over her shoulder.

"No. Jason." She grinned. "I'm reaching out for that ride of a lifetime Carly promised me!" She grabbed the suitcase and started for the front door. "Oh, tell Mitch I'll return the car next week, if I can buy my own car by then!" She called over her shoulder.

"Did I miss something?" She heard her aunt ask Carly as she left the house.

She stowed the bags in the trunk and then drove over to Jack's office. He must have heard her pull into the lot because he was waiting in the reception area when she walked through the door, a smile on his face.

"About time you got your butt over here," he indicated for her to head into his office. "Well, I guess I don't have to ask what your decision was. That rock announces it to the world for you."

"What would you say if I told you that Jason and I agreed that the commute wouldn't kill either of us?" She raised her eyebrows, sitting back in her chair.

"If I thought you wanted to go back to that life, I'd say 'good for you'. Since I know you don't, I'd ask what drugs you were taking when you agreed to that," Jack leaned back and propped his feet on his desk. "Are you staying?"

"I'm staying, and yes, Jason and I are getting married. And, if your offer was a legitimate one, I'd like to take you up on it," she found herself smiling over at him.

Jack grunted and handed over a file. "As if I'd go through the hassle of making a non-legitimate offer. Here, this all that tax crap you have to fill out in order to get on my payroll. You can start in two weeks. The offer letter is on top," he grinned as she took the file from him. "Damn, but it'll be good to have you around. No one else can think as fast with the comebacks as you can."

"So you're hiring me for my ability to give back the shit you toss around all day? No wonder Stacy is never around." Standing up, she walked around the desk to give him a hug. "Thanks, Jack. You know just how to make a girl feel special."

"You're welcome, kid." he gave her a quick grin and a wink. "Now get out of here so I can get my work done."

With a laugh, she headed out the door. She headed into town, stopping at the grocery store to pick up the ingredients to make dinner for Jason, and then headed to his place. She carried her purchases into the kitchen, and put everything away, and then took her bags into the bedroom. She hesitated for a second before emptying out one of his dresser drawers for her things, and hanging up a few items in the closet. She took a deep breath and released it. This was what she wanted. She just had to continue to have faith that it would all work out.

CHAPTER 23

Nicole made sure she had everything put away in the bedroom. She wanted to surprise Jason with her decision to move in with him. Glancing at the clock, she realized it was time to get dinner in the oven. It wasn't anything fancy, but she remembered what Jason liked to eat. Quick and easy, those were her favorite dinners to cook.

A little before five, she took a glass of wine and the file Jack had given her and stepped out onto the deck. She settled herself into one of the lounge chairs and looked over the offer and started filling out the paperwork. God, she hated all these tax forms.

A shadow fell over her papers, and she glanced up to find Jason standing over her.

"Hi," she smiled up at him. "How long have you been home?"

"I just got home. I was a little confused when I couldn't find you inside," he sat down next to her legs on the chair. "How long have *you* been here?"

"I got here around one, I guess. I, uh, made you dinner." Closing the file, she started to stand up but stopped when he put his hand on her arm.

"I didn't mean to make you uncomfortable this morning, and I'm trying very hard not to push," he took her hand and linked his fingers with hers. "I just don't want to lose you again."

She reached over with her free hand and caressed his face. "I know. And I don't mean to be difficult, but this..." she waved her hand to indicate the two of them, "this is very scary for me. I'm not trying to stall, and I'm not running away. I've told you what my mother was like, but now everything I ever believed about my childhood is in question. If I remember right, you grew up in a house full of love. I just need time to get used to all of this."

Leaning forward, he stopped her with a kiss. "It's okay, Cole. We can try to slow down. *I* can try to slow down. I just need to know you're as committed to us as I am," he gave her another kiss, this one lingering for a few extra seconds. "And I need you to share what you're thinking. I'm not a mind reader, you know," he stood up and pulled her to her feet. "What's in the folder?"

"The offer letter from Jack and all the paperwork I'm supposed to fill out to get on the payroll. I start in two weeks," she followed him inside and set the folder on the counter.

"How soon will dinner be ready?" he asked as he grabbed a bottle of water from the refrigerator.

"About twenty minutes," she told him, checking the oven. "You have enough time to go change and relax for a few minutes."

"I'm going to go take a quick shower, then," he stepped over beside her and kissed her.

Nicole was smiling as he walked away. That man could kiss, no doubt about that. She sighed and turned to finish making their dinner, trying to keep her thoughts on what she was doing, not what he would look like naked, in the shower, with water running over him. Shaking herself out of her daydreams, she grabbed the bread knife and started slicing the loaf of French bread she'd bought.

Twenty minutes later, he strode back into the kitchen, giving an appreciative sniff. "Something smells good."

"Perfect timing," she commented, glancing over at him. His hair was still damp and he'd shaved. Pity. She enjoyed feeling the stubble of his beard on her skin.

"Can you grab the veggies?" she paused when his arms came around her waist.

"I noticed the clothes hanging in the closet. I take it the decision to move in with me has been made?"

Nicole turned into his embrace and laid her head on his chest, her arms encircling his waist. "I thought that...I am committed to us, Jason. This was my way of trying to meet you halfway."

He tilted her face up so he could look in her eyes. "I like it," he kissed the tip of her nose and let her go. After helping her put the rest of their meal on the table, he waited for her to sit down before he joined her. "This looks good," he reached for the chicken. "So, besides moving a few things over here from the ranch and cooking dinner for us, what did you do all day?"

"By the time I went to the ranch, packed up a few things, drove to Jack's office and then made a stop at the store, I didn't have time to do much else before starting dinner. I decided to start filling out all the tax forms right before you got home."

"Is the offer worth it?" he glanced at the folder she'd left on the counter.

"You can look it over, if you want to. It's not quite the six figure salary I'd make in Austin, but it's a solid offer," turning in her chair, she reached over and snagged the folder. "The health insurance is better than I had in Austin, believe it or not, and the cost of living will be cheaper here. He's offering me a full partnership in his business," she watched him as he read the letter. "Besides, you're here. That makes up for anything else," she finished, earning herself a smile from him.

"Is the money that important to you?" Setting the folder aside, he resumed eating his dinner.

"Not at all. I want enough to be able to send my children to the college of their choice without worrying about it, and I'd like to be able to do all the fun stuff we want to do, without having to worry about where that money will come from. But in all honesty, I've never touched the money my parents left me, and Uncle Steve's had his investment team looking over it for me all these years, so I have a nice little nest egg already built up," she revealed. They'd never talked about finances. She wasn't sure how he'd feel about all of this information.

Pushing his plate away, he stretched his legs out in front of him and leaned back in his chair. "Yeah, I use the same firm. They're an excellent team, great at what they do. They've built up quite the portfolio for me, as well. And speaking of good, dinner was excellent. Thank you," he leaned across the table to kiss her. "Since you cooked, I'll clean up."

"Okay," she agreed with a smile. Standing up, he gave her a wink and started clearing the table. She watched him in silence for a few minutes.

"Tell me about your childhood," she invited.

"What?" startled, he glanced up from putting the dishes in the dishwasher.

"In all the time we spent together in college, we never talked about ourselves, at least, not our pasts. I mean, I knew both of your parents were dead, like mine, and I knew you and Mitch had met in Austin while you were doing part of your residency. But other than that, I don't know anything about you," her eyes followed his movements as he added soap to the dishwasher and closed the door. Rinsing off his hands, he turned to face her as he dried them on a towel.

"Come on," he reached over and snagged her hand and led her to the living room. Sitting down on the sofa, he pulled her down beside him.

"Jason..."

"I promise we'll talk. I just like having you close," he explained as he wrapped his arm around her shoulders. As he started talking, she laid her head on his shoulder. "I grew up near Houston. My dad worked for NASA, and my mom was a housewife. There were some complications with her pregnancy and so I wound up being an only child."

"When did she die?"

"I was eight years old. Old enough to understand what death was, but not old enough to understand why. It was cancer, and she fought it for as long as she could, but her body just couldn't take anymore," he closed his eyes.

"Dad remarried about two years after her death. I was too young to resent Janet, and she was nice enough to me," his voice trailed off as he thought of his step-mother. "Anyway, Dad and Janet had a little girl together, Bayleigh, who is a couple of years younger than you. She was a real handful when she was in her teens and caused Janet a lot of grief, from what Janet told me. Bayleigh ran off a couple of months after her high school graduation, hooked up with some singer in a band. They thought they'd do better in England, so they've been over there for the last couple of years. They're signed to be an opening act for some band over there. We keep in touch by email for the most part, an occasional phone call when we can get the time difference right."

Jason leaned his head back against the sofa, staring at the ceiling. "Dad developed some heart problems and had a few minor heart attacks, which forced him to retire. He just gave up after that. He died when I was twenty-four. Janet died just a few years ago, complications from diabetes." They sat in silence for a few minutes, before Nicole sat up.

"I never had that," she told him. At his inquisitive look, she continued. "Those secure feelings of knowing both of your parents loved you, or were even proud of you. I knew my dad loved me, and he was always there when I needed to talk out my childhood problems, and he was proud of my grades. But my mom..." She had to swallow hard around the lump filling her throat. "My mom, she never wasted an opportunity to tell me how I shouldn't let boys distract me, reminding me love was an illusion. I don't remember her ever holding me or offering me comfort in any way. After reading that letter, I guess I kind of get it. But now I'm furious with my dad.

"Before, I hadn't cared that she was gone. It was easier to just be relieved that she wasn't there to always knock me down. But now..." she paused to take a deep breath. "Now, I have all these questions about who my birth father was, and who was she running off with, and why did my dad not only kill her but himself, too?"

"Would it change anything if you could get those answers?" he cocked his head to the side.

"Depends on what you mean. If I had names, I might be able to get some closure on all of this. Would it change how I reacted to certain situations? I doubt it. I think I still would have been hesitant to admit to being in love," she admitted.

"So, how *did* you convince yourself to take that leap and allow yourself to fall in love with me?" he asked pulling her back into the comfort of his arms.

"Somehow, you managed to break through those barriers I had up. There was always that part of me that thought: what if she was right and love was just an illusion? Not being loved by my own parent was bad enough, and I had no choice in who my parents were. But I could choose whether or not to fall in love, and not have to risk being rejected a second time," she laid her hand on his thigh. "But then I met my cousin's best friend."

"And he scared the crap out of you and you spent years running in the opposite direction," he supplied.

"I guess that's one way of putting it," she agreed, grimacing. "Jason, have you ever thought about what might have happened if you had pushed me a little harder and had slept with me?"

He made her sit up and positioned himself so they were facing each other. "Yeah, I thought about it a lot. I thought about seducing you, and getting you pregnant and making you marry me. Hell, all I would have had to do was spend the night and let Mitch catch me in your room; whether or not we'd had sex would have been irrelevant. He would have been on the phone with Steve, Helen, with Jack conferenced in, within moments of that kind of discovery. The four of them would have overridden any objections you had."

"Why didn't you?" she asked, wide-eyed, not realizing he'd ever put so much thought into it before.

"One simple reason: I would have lost you anyway," he took her hands in his. "You didn't tell me about your parents, or your mom's twisted views back then, but some of the comments you did make...I knew someone had screwed you up somewhere along the line. I knew if I took the choice away from you, you'd hate me. I had to accept the fact that you wanted different things out of life," he reached over and touched her cheek with his fingers. "Or you thought you did."

She leaned over and gave him a soft kiss. "I thought I did. Now all I want is a life with you," she told him. "I want everything you mentioned a few days ago including a few children."

"I think I can manage to accommodate you," he teased, pulling her back into his arms. "When should we start?"

"Not until after October. I would like to be married

before we start trying to build you a dynasty," Nicole smiled at him.

"Who said we're getting married in October? I thought you wanted a December wedding?"

"October would be meeting halfway," she told him, earning another kiss. They continued to sit on the couch, discussing their future together and making simple plans. If only things could always be this easy and simple.

CHAPTER 24

N icole couldn't believe how much work needed to be done for a wedding. God bless Aunt Helen and Carly. Those two women swept in and Nicole allowed them to take over. All she had to do was say "Yes" or "No" to their ideas. From there, she and Jason just had to show up when they were told to.

The church was reserved for the first Saturday in November and Aunt Helen was counting on the weather still being warm enough for an outside reception. Everything was falling into place. Now they just had to get all the little details taken care of. Nicole hated the little details.

She and Jack had settled into an easy working routine. Nicole had found she didn't miss her big city, high-class law firm job and quite enjoyed being able to review a contract for the sale of a bull one minute, and then switching gears and working on a will the next. And working with her best friend, well, that was priceless.

She was sitting at her computer in her "corner office"

one day when Jason stuck his head through the doorway, surprising her. "Hey, beautiful."

"Hey, yourself," Nicole pushed back from her desk and met him halfway across the room for a kiss. "What are you doing here at this time of day? Don't you have patients?"

"Nope, my two o'clock cancelled, and my three o'clock meeting at the hospital was cancelled, so I cut out early. I thought you might want to play hooky with me?"

"I don't think the slave driver will let me go," she jerked her head in the direction of Jack's office.

"I heard that!" Jack called out.

"What do you say, old buddy? Can I take my girl out of here for the afternoon?" Jason called over his shoulder before turning to wink at Nicole.

Jack came out of his office, muttering under his breath, but she caught the grin on his face he was trying to hide.

"I'm not sure you two deserve any breaks," he clapped Jason on the shoulder in greeting. "Hell, I already give her weekends off, and now you want me to let her go before quitting time on a Friday afternoon? She's already getting to take a honeymoon."

"See? Slave Driver!" Nicole pulled a rubber band off her wrist and aimed it at Jack and let it fly.

"Hey! Isn't there a law against abusing your employer?" Jack caught the rubber band and shot it back at her.

"I can see you two get a lot done around here," Jason chuckled, stepping in front of Nicole to block her next shot. He ignored Nicole's pout as he took the rubber band away from her before reaching across the desk to grab her purse.

"She started it," Jack pointed over at her and she stuck her tongue out at him. "See what I put up with? You go ahead and get her out of here, maybe knock some respect into her for me, will you?" Jack stepped back out of the way so Jason could lead her out of the room.

"Thanks, Jack. I'll see you on Tuesday!" she called over her shoulder on a laugh as she was pulled down the hallway.

"Where are we going, anyway?" she asked, still laughing, when they reached his truck. "And what am I going to do about my car?"

"Your car will be safe here. We'll come back and get it later, or we can call over to the ranch and have Steve and one of the ranch hands get it," he started the truck and pulled out of the parking lot.

"They've got the frame for the house done. I thought you might like to see it, and then we're going to meet Carly and Mitch in Austin for a late dinner and some fun. I've got a bag in the back with everything we need for a night out on the town."

"Sounds like fun," she agreed, leaning her head back against the headrest. "Have you already been by to see it?"

"Nope. I waited for you. What's that guy's name...Bill? He called this morning, said they had the framing done and had started putting up the exterior siding and whatnot. So if they stay on schedule, they'll be doing the interior work in just a few more weeks. He wants to be sure we haven't made any changes to our plans."

"Did he say how much longer until it's done?"

"We should be able to move in around the holidays, it'll just depend on the weather for the next few weeks, and how fast he can get people out here to do the building inspections when the time comes," he made the turn onto her property and drove down to the site they'd picked out for the house.

It was in the same general area as the old house had been, since that ground was already pretty level, but she hadn't wanted their new house to be in the exact same spot. She had vetoed that suggestion the very second it was suggested.

"Hey, Jason, Nicole. What do you think?" Bill, the site foreman, walked over to greet them and they shook hands. "The boys are taking a short break, so if you want to look around, you can."

"Do you want to go in?" Jason asked. At her nod, he took her hand to help her over some of the debris. They walked through the house, looking at the progress that had been made in the last couple of weeks since they'd last been out to look at it.

"Well?" Bill walked up to them after they finished looking at everything.

"Looks good, Bill. Thanks. You still think December before it's done? Nicole asked, looking around.

"We're still on schedule, so yeah, I'd say mid-December at the latest," he tapped the rolled up blueprints he always seemed to be carrying. "We're working as fast and hard as we can."

"I know. I appreciate it," she smiled her thanks at him. It wasn't like they didn't have anywhere to stay. Jason wasn't going to sell his condo until they had a firm date on the house being done. She watched Jason step over to talk to Bill about one of the questions he had about the wiring in what was going to be their home office. She couldn't believe how everything was working out.

"You ready to go, babe?" Jason stepped back over to her, wrapping an arm around her waist.

She smiled and leaned into the embrace for a second. "I'm ready when you are," she answered. He kissed the top of her head and they headed back to his truck.

"So where are we going now?" she asked, placing her hand in his when he reached across the seats.

"We are going to go to dinner with our friends, and then find somewhere to go dancing. Carly told Mitch she needed a night away from the ranch, and I thought we could use a night away, too." Jason gave her hand a quick squeeze.

She nodded her agreement, and they rode in silence for a while, listening to the radio and making small talk. She updated him about the plans for the reception dinner. Jason had been as ready and willing to turn everything over to Helen and Carly as she'd been. As long as the end result was they got to say "I do," and Nicole would be his forever, he didn't care about the details.

They checked in at the hotel first. She headed for the bathroom to reapply her makeup and change into the clothes Jason had picked out for her. She heard him turn on the television and start flipping channels.

She checked her reflection in the mirror, and gave a wry grin. He'd picked out the tightest fitting jeans she owned along with a sleeveless, low cut shirt that hugged her in all the right places. Open the door, she found him lounging on the king size bed, all the pillows stacked behind his head.

"Oh, God. Even better than I imagined," he growled, sitting up when she walked over and reaching out his hand to pull her down beside him, his mouth covering hers. "Do you think Mitch and Carly would mind if we're late?" he asked, his voice low and seductive, his hands already moving underneath the shirt.

"You are insatiable!" she laughed, returning his kiss. "But Carly gets mean and pissy now if she doesn't get fed on time," she pushed him back. "I'll make it up to you, tonight. I promise," she gave him a quick kiss. "Where are we meeting them, anyway?"

"Spoil sport," Jason grumbled, getting off the bed. "Over by the Arboretum. Carly wanted to go to The Cheesecake Factory over there, and then there's some new country bar with live music she wanted to go to," Jason headed into the bathroom with his shaving kit. "At least we have a built in designated driver!"

She pushed herself off the bed and leaned against the door of the bathroom to watch him shave. He'd taken off his shirt, and her eyes roamed over his broad shoulders and chest, down to his tight abdomen.

His eyes met hers in the mirror and he gave her a wink. "Or you could plead a headache, or something, and I could stay here to tend to your needs," he suggested with a playful leer.

"Uh-huh. Tend to your own needs, you mean," she teased. "Nope, I want to go see this new bar. One of the hands was up here last weekend and his wife told us about it. It sounds fun, and the band they have right now is awesome, she said."

He stepped over in front of her, wiping the shaving cream off of his face with one of the towels. "You really know how to knock a man down," he told her, leaning over to give her a kiss.

She grinned up at him and hooked her fingers into his belt loops and pulled him up against her. "Isn't there some old saying about always leave 'em wantin' more?" she asked him, feeling his ready response. He grabbed her hips and held her tight against him and kissed her senseless. She was on the verge of telling him to forget their friends when he broke off the kiss and pushed her hips away from his.

"That works both ways, darlin'," he told her, grabbing his clean shirt off the hanger and shrugging into it. "You might want to check your hair." He grinned at her, letting her know with just that look that he knew how close she'd been to changing her mind. He moved over to the bed, sitting down to pull on his boots.

She shot him a disgruntled look and stepped into the bathroom to run a brush through her hair. She grabbed her purse and found her lipstick, and slicked some on her lips. "How do I look?" she turned to find him staring at her.

"Gorgeous," he stood up and walked over to her, brushing a few errant strands of hair back away from her face. "Let's go find our friends, before I decide to hold you hostage." They walked side by side to the elevator and headed out for their night of adventure.

CHAPTER 25

"Wow, this place is awesome, with a capital 'a'!" Carly had to lean over and shout to be heard above the music. "You and Jason look good out there," Carly grinned over at her while Nicole glanced around at the crowd. They had been lucky to snag one of the corner booths, and she and Jason had spent most of the evening on the dance floor, and Nicole was ready to take a break. She'd sent Jason and Mitch up to the bar for refills.

"Thanks. You and Mitch don't look too bad yourselves," Nicole smiled up at Jason as he and Mitch slid into the booth next to the women and handed them their drinks. There was a break in the music as the band finished their set and the dance floor emptied. The music was switched back to the jukebox which wasn't as loud as the band had been, so people could now talk without yelling.

"You doing okay? Your back isn't bothering you, is it?" he asked, his lips against her ear, making her shiver, as his hand settled on her thigh.

She shook her head, reaching up with her free hand to

brush a lock of hair off his forehead. "You worry too much," she told him, leaning her head against his shoulder, turning her attention back to her cousins. Mitch was asking about the progress of their house, and Nicole let Jason fill them in on the details.

Just a few more weeks – eight to be exact – and they would be married. She sighed with contentment, rubbing her cheek against him as his fingers tightened on her thigh. Nicole let her gaze wander around the other tables, noticing all the couples, sitting much as she and Jason, and Mitch and Carly, for that matter, were so close some parts of their bodies were touching each other, and heads tilted to catch the words as they were spoken.

His hand left her thigh and he placed it on the back of the booth, his fingers cupping her shoulder. She felt him turn his head just enough to press a kiss to her head. Half listening to the conversation at their table, she again let her eyes wander over the crowd. Not quite believing what she saw, she sat up, her eyes wide.

"What?" Jason looked over at her and followed her gaze.

"That's Peter over there," she indicated a table a short distance away.

"Peter? As in the jackass who stole your promotion?" Carly leaned around Mitch to study the other man.

The other man chose just that moment to look up and his eyes met Nicole's. His eyes widened and he leaned across the table to speak to the others he was with and then he stood up and walked over to their table.

"Nicole! How are you, honey? I heard you were coming back to town to take over my old job," he glanced at the other three and nodded, dismissing them as unimportant with a look.

"Peter," Nicole greeted him, her voice cold as ice, as she rested her hand on Jason's thigh and gave him a warning squeeze as she felt his fingers contract on her shoulder. "You heard wrong. I won't be returning to work for Robert. I've had a better offer back home." She gave him a cool smile and then indicated her cousins. "This is my cousin, Mitch, and his wife Carly." She raised her hand and placed it on Jason's chest, making sure the diamond on her ring finger sparkled. "And this is Jason Morrow, my fiancé."

"Fiancé?" Peter looked down his nose at the other man. "You must not mind icicles."

"I just know how to make them melt," Jason returned, his voice hard. Nicole glanced up at him and saw the tight reign he had on his temper. A muscle worked in Peter's jaw as he stared down at them.

"You turned Robert down?" he glanced back at Nicole.

"I did. As I said, I had a better offer." Nicole took a sip of her drink, amazed that her hand wasn't shaking.

She glanced over at the stage. "Oh, look, honey. The band is going to start up again. Let's go dance a little more before we head back to our room."

Jack nodded, tossing back the rest of his own drink, but Peter was blocking their exit from the booth. Jason frowned at the other man. "Do you mind?"

"She's frigid, you know. She'll tease you until you're crazy with it, and then just turn it off...oaf" Peter found himself sitting on the floor.

Jason slid out of the booth and reached back to give

Nicole a hand. Startled, she realized he had managed to hook an ankle around Peter to make him fall.

"Man, you have got to be careful on these floors! They get so slippery if someone spills a drink," Jason wrapped his arm around Nicole's waist. "If you'll excuse us, my fiancé and I are going to go enjoy the band some more before we head back to our hotel." He glared down at the other man, who was flushed, whether from anger or embarrassment, Nicole wasn't sure. Peter was slow to pull himself to his feet, glaring at the four of them before heading back to his own table.

"You guys going to hang around for a while?" Jason's eyes followed Peter but his question was for Mitch.

"Naw, little momma here is about to fall asleep. I'm going to finish this beer and then we'll head out. We'll catch you for breakfast tomorrow, though," Mitch leaned back, his arm around his wife. "I'll watch your back for a few, before we leave."

Nicole smiled her own thanks to her cousin and followed Jason out to the dance floor. The band was playing a soft love song to start off their next set, and she settled into his arms with a sigh.

"I'm sorry," she whispered, wrapping her arms around him.

"For what?" he gave a gentle tug on her hair to make her look at him. "Honey, that jackass is the one who needs to apologize. He was just trying to make trouble," he bent his head towards her and gave her a gentle kiss. "Now, if you're apologizing for ever going out with someone like that to begin with when you had me waiting back in Waketon, well, then I guess you do owe me an apology at that," he teased.

"What did I ever do to deserve you?" she whispered, her fingers teasing the hair on his neck. "Will you do something for me?"

"Anything." he assured her, his eyes glancing around the room to make sure Peter wasn't going to try to start anymore trouble.

"Take me back to the hotel and show me how un-frigid I am?"

He pulled back and looked into her eyes, seeing the pain that that one statement had created. He gave her another gentle kiss and then led her from the dance floor. They walked over to their table, where Mitch was just finishing his beer, and he glanced up at them, eyebrows raised.

"Everything okay?" Mitch asked, his concerned eyes catching hers.

"We're fine. We've just decided that we're ready to go, too." Jason reached down and grabbed Nicole's purse off the table. "You guys going to be okay to get back to the hotel?"

"Yup. I only nursed those two beers, same as you." Mitch stood up and then reached down to help his wife to her feet. "Do ya'll want to meet at ten for breakfast?" They nodded their agreement and the two couples headed for the door.

Jason drove them back downtown to their hotel and left his truck with the valet parking. He wrapped his arm around Nicole's waist and led her to the bank of elevators. The elevator stopped on their floor, and he escorted her down the hallway to their room. He opened the door for her and waited for her to enter before him. She walked over to the windows, and stared out at the city around her.

"You okay?" he wrapped his arms around her waist from behind her, pulling her back against him.

"I'm fine." she assured him, relaxing against him, feeling his strength. "Thank you," she leaned her head against his shoulder.

"For what? I didn't do anything, except knock that pompous pretty boy on his ass." She laughed at Jason's description.

"Thank you for that, too," she turned in his arms and slipped her arms up around his neck. "Ever since I left you, there have been a number of men like Peter, who even if they didn't choose those words, accused me of being frigid," she laid her fingers over his mouth when she sensed he was going to interrupt her. "I had even begun to believe it might be true. I just could never respond to them. I'd hear my mother's voice in my head, and I'd just freeze up. No matter what I tried, I'd just freeze up." She laid her head on his chest and felt his arms wrap around her, holding her close.

"So what's different now? I mean, you pulled back that first night, but I wouldn't say you froze," he asked, his lips moving against her ear.

"With you, there was always something different. Maybe I was too immature to recognize it for what it was, but now I know, and I believe in it, and in you," she leaned back in his arms and looked up at him, meeting his intense look. "You love me, and I love you."

"That's what I've been telling you," he agreed, smiling down at her.

She smiled back and tugged his mouth down to hers. "Thank you for being patient with me, for loving me, then and now," she whispered against his mouth, her fingers going to the buttons on his shirt.

He worked his hands under her sweater, undoing the front clasp of her bra, his thumbs brushing over her nipples. She moaned tearing her mouth away from his, pushing his shirt down his arms, placing soft kisses against his chest. He worked his arms out of his sleeves, his own mouth working its magic against the sensitive area below her ear, down to her collarbone. He picked her up in his arms and carried her over to the bed. He made quick work of the remainder of their clothes before joining her, his warm body covering hers. He levered himself up on his elbows, his eyes catching and holding hers.

"You are mine and I love you, now and forever," he told her, caressing her face with his hands, while hers danced over his spine.

"And I'll love you forever," she whispered on a moan as he filled her, pushing all other thoughts from her mind. Now was not the time for doubts.

CHAPTER 26

Nicole hated being home alone. After years of living by herself, and traveling so much for the job, it had surprised her how much she loved having sharing her space. Of course, part of that was just the fact that she loved who she was sharing that space with. But for the next three nights, she was alone.

Jason was attending a medical conference in Houston and had left that morning. He had promised to call her but so far, she hadn't heard from him. She'd picked up the phone to call him countless times, but each time hung up before the call went through. She refused to be one of those clingy women. Patience was not one of her virtues.

With a heavy sigh, she tried to refocus on the contract in her lap. Right now, she didn't care about the sale of her client's prize bull. And the buyer had a list of demands she was having to go through and research to see if they were legitimate or not. Already, she had a page of notes she needed to talk to the seller about and see what he thought.

With a groan, she tossed her notebook and pen on the

coffee table and glanced at the clock. Ten o'clock. Where *was* he?

The phone rang, and she grabbed the handset before the first ring had even finished. "Jason? Are you okay?" So much for playing it cool.

"Hi, sweetheart," he chuckled at her eager greeting. "I guess you miss me."

"A little, I was starting to get worried," she admitted. "Did you get there okay?"

"I'm fine. I ran into an old friend when I was checking in and we decided to have a few drinks after the presentation tonight. I just got back to my room," he yawned. "Christ, it has been a long day."

"For me, too. I'm sitting here reviewing a contract for the sale of a bull," she told him. "What time do you start tomorrow?"

"Early. They're serving breakfast at seven-thirty, and the lectures start at nine. We'll finish up for the day around five-thirty, and then another dinner meeting," he yawned again. They talked for a few minutes before he pleaded exhaustion.

Nicole hung up the phone and got ready for bed. Not able to fall asleep, she laid there in the dark, staring up at the ceiling. She had heard a slight hesitation in Jason's voice a couple of times during their brief conversation, and now she wasn't quite sure what to think. He had sounded tired, and she didn't doubt he was; after all, he had chosen to drive to Houston and it was at least a six hour drive. But he hadn't even said he missed her or loved her.

Groaning, she grabbed Jason's pillow and hugged it to her chest. *"It's just pre-wedding jitters. I've got six weeks until the wedding and I'm just panicking,*" she inhaled his scent from the pillow. But the doubts plagued her all night. She was still worrying about it the next morning when she arrived at the office. She knew she looked as bad as she felt but she was hoping work would keep her mind away from those nagging thoughts.

"Nicole, did you get a chance...you okay?" Jack stopped in the doorway to her office.

"I'm fine, I just had trouble sleeping last night," she handed over the file she knew he was getting ready to ask her for. "I made comments in the margin for you."

Jack glanced at a couple of her notes and nodded, snapping the folder shut and then looking back up at her. "Do you need to talk about it? I know Jason's out of town until Sunday," he offered, and she smiled at him.

"Thanks, but I'm just being silly and reading into something that isn't even there. You know, nervous bride kind of stuff," she leaned back in her chair and narrowed her gaze. "Speaking of which, have you gotten measured for your tux yet?"

"I've got a client waiting..." Jack started to back out of the room.

"Jack!" Nicole called after him, a warning in her tone. "Don't make me sorry I asked you to be the one to walk me down that aisle!"

"Today, I promise!" he called over his shoulder.

Chuckling, she pulled up her client's file and reached for the phone. It was time to put those lingering doubts out of her mind and get to work.

She spent the day writing up the contracts for the sale of the prize bull for their client, ironing out the details between the buyer and seller. As soon as the contracts were signed, she dragged Jack to the tuxedo shop to ensure that he was fitted, like he had promised, and then she went out to the ranch for dinner with her family. Carly and Helen had even more wedding stuff to go over.

It was after nine o'clock before she got back to the condo. She had tried to call Jason twice during the evening, leaving messages on both his cell phone and at the hotel, letting him know where she was, but he didn't return either call. But he had told her that between the conference sessions, and then the dinner meetings, he was going to be pretty busy.

Glancing at the answering machine, she was disappointed to see that the light was not blinking. No calls. She headed for the bathroom to take a long, hot shower, hoping to ease some of the tension in her neck and shoulders, letting the water beat down on her, until she at least felt a little more relaxed.

She grabbed her robe off the hook by the shower door, slid into it, wandering out to the kitchen to get a cup of herbal tea, hoping it would do its trick and relax her. She glanced over at the clock and sighed. Who was she kidding? If she didn't talk to him soon, she was going to lose her mind.

She grabbed the handset off its base and once again dialed Jason's cell phone. Again, it went straight to voice mail, and she hung up without leaving a message. She dialed the hotel and asked for his room, and the clerk put her call through.

"Hello?" a soft voice answered the phone.

She pulled the phone away from her ear and stared at

it, and then disconnected the call. She called the front desk again and the same clerk answered.

"I'm sorry, I was trying to reach Doctor Jason Morrow, and I think I was connected to the wrong room. Could you try again, please?" she tapped her fingers on the kitchen counter while the call was transferred.

The same soft, very female, voice answered the phone.

"I'm sorry. I'm trying to reach Doctor Jason Morrow?" Nicole hated how hesitant that came out. "The front desk transferred me to this number."

"He's in the shower," the voice informed her.

"Who is this?" her heart was pounding and now she felt sick to her stomach.

"Doctor Sara Douglas. Who is this?"

"Doctor...I'm sorry, did you say *Sara*?" she was almost afraid that the handset was going to disintegrate in her hand as her grip tightened.

"Yes, and who *is* this?" Sara's tone was impatient.

"This is his fiancé. Or maybe I should say ex-fiancé. Please tell Jason...Never mind." She hung up the phone and slammed it down on the counter, wanting to scream. This could not be happening. The wedding was only a few weeks away! The phone rang, but knowing it was *him*, she ignored it.

"Nicole, pick up the phone. I know you're there. Nicole, please, baby, talk to me. Nicole?" Jason's voice sounded over the answering machine. "Honey, just let me explain..."

Nicole reached over and turned the volume down so she didn't have to listen to it. She went into the bedroom and grabbed a pair of jeans and a shirt, yanking them on.

Throwing some clothes into her suitcase, she ignored the ringing phone.

She grabbed her keys and purse off the kitchen counter and headed for her car. Now her cell phone was ringing as well. As she dug it out of her purse, she looked at the caller ID.

You think I'm going to pick up after that shit? She hit the 'ignore button and then turned the phone off. The suitcase was tossed into the trunk and then she slid into the driver's seat.

Within thirty minutes after having Doctor Sara Douglas answer *her* fiancé's phone, Nicole pulled up in front of Jack's house. Luck was on her side, as his lights were still on, and she saw movement in the living room. The front door opened and he stepped out on the porch as she opened her car door.

"Nicole? Is everything okay?" He reached behind him and hit the switch to turn on the floodlights. She swallowed hard and raised her hand in greeting. "Nicole?" Jack started down the porch steps and met her halfway between the house and car. "Is it Jason?"

That was all it took for the tears to start. "He's a lying bastard!" she managed to sob, as Jack wrapped his arm around her shoulders and led her back into his house. Leading her to one of the kitchen chairs, he grabbed a bottle of whiskey and a glass off the counter, and a couple of paper napkins out of the dispenser, and set everything in front of her.

"I'm sorry." She took a deep breath and tried to get the tears to stop as Jack poured a couple of fingers worth of the whiskey into the glass and pushed it across the table to her.

She held the glass between her palms and stared at the amber liquid. Jack sat down across from her and waited.

"Drink it, Nicole, and then tell me what he did."

She tossed the whiskey back, coughing as it burned its way down her throat. She coughed a few times, grabbing one of the napkins to wipe at her eyes. "I hadn't heard from Jason all day and I'd left him a couple of messages, so when I got home from dinner, I decided to try one more time. Sara Douglas answered the phone in his hotel room."

"Sara...oh shit," Jack leaned back. "Did you talk to Jason?"

"No, I hung up and I wouldn't answer the phone when he tried to call back. I had to get out of there," she looked across the table at him. "I didn't know where else to go. I'm sure he's already called over to the ranch."

"I'm sure there's a reasonable explanation," he started to say.

"For my fiancé to have another woman in the hotel room after ten o'clock at night, while he's in the shower? How reasonable do you want me to be?" Nicole's voice was hard.

"He'd better be careful showing his face around here. Mitch and Pop will shoot him and bury the body somewhere on Pop's four hundred acres," Jack leaned forward and grabbed the whiskey bottle, pouring himself a shot. "You know you can stay here if you want." He tilted the bottle towards her, "More?"

She shook her head as Jack's cellphone rang. He glanced at the screen as he picked up the phone. "It's Mitch," he informed her, answering it.

She stared at the worn tabletop, tracing designs in the

wood as she half listened to Jack filling Mitch in on the situation. It was obvious from the one-sided conversation she'd been right and Jason had already called over to the ranch.

"She'll stay here tonight, but she doesn't want to talk to him right now," a minute later, Jack hung up the phone. "He says to let them know if you need anything."

"I just need time," she sighed, rubbing her hands over her face.

Jack stood up, "Listen, you don't need to decide the rest of your life tonight. Stay here tonight and tomorrow morning you can go down to San Antonio for me."

"San Antonio?" she raised her eyes to his, confusion radiating from them.

"I'm supposed to go to that conference down there this weekend, remember? You go in my place. I won't tell anyone who where you are," Jack offered.

"I don't feel like going to the conference."

"So don't go to the conference, just go hang out in San Antonio, see the sights," Jack stopped by her chair and put his hand on her shoulder. "Take some time to think it all through. I can handle your clients for a few days."

She nodded her agreement and watched Jack head down the hallway. "You know where the guest room is, and the towels!" He called over his shoulder as he headed into his room.

She waved to show him she heard and then stood up. The lights were still on in the living room, so she turned those off for him before heading to the guest room. The rest of the night was spent crying into the pillow until the break of dawn, calling Jason every foul name she could think of. As the first rays of the morning sun were streaking across the sky, she got out of bed and headed out to the kitchen, where Jack was already up, drinking his coffee.

"So, what did you decide?" he asked, his sharp eyes taking in her swollen eyes, and the dark circles underneath.

"I'm going to San Antonio," she reached for a mug and poured herself a cup of the coffee, grimacing as she took in the dark color. Jack liked his coffee strong.

"Will you be back?"

"Yes. I'm not a quitter, Jack. I might not be getting married in a few weeks, but I'm not leaving Waketon again," she dumped sugar and cream into the coffee and took a tentative sip. Jack grinned at the face she made.

"What do you need me to do?"

"I'm sure, knowing Jason, he'll be back sometime today to try and patch things up with me. Just don't let him know where I've gone." She waited for Jack to nod his agreement. "I'm going to leave here and drive straight down there. Can you just call the hotel and change the reservation to my name please?"

Jack grabbed a pen and paper off the counter and wrote the name of the hotel down for her. "It's on the River Walk." The itinerary and the slip of paper with the hotel's information on it were slid across the table to her. "Stay as long as you need to, my treat. Should I tell Carly and Helen where you've gone?"

"Just please ask them to not tell Jason. I'm not sure when I'll be ready to talk to him," she took another swallow of the coffee, and then dumped it down the sink, causing Jack to chuckle.

"Sorry. I used my usual amount out of habit. Do you want me to make another pot?"

"No, I'll do it," she grabbed the coffee and filters and started a fresh pot. "How do you stand it that strong?"

"How do you stand it that weak?" he shot back, standing up. "You want some breakfast?"

She stood back and watched him start making omelets. Feeling her eyes on him, he glanced over.

"What?" he reached back into the refrigerator and grabbed the cheese and mushrooms. "You can make some toast, if you're not too busy watching the coffee drip."

She took the loaf of bread out of the bread box and moved over to the toaster. "I was just wondering...you told me that one day you'd lost the only woman you'd ever loved. Why didn't you ever try again with someone else?"

For a minute, she didn't think he was going to answer her. He turned the heat down under the omelets and turned to look at her. "I was bitter, for a long time, for starters. I had thought I'd loved her and I thought she felt the same way." The toast popped up and he watched as she buttered it and set it on a plate.

"I tell myself I was lucky I found out what she was like before I fell into her trap." Jack slid the omelets out onto plates and set them down on the table. "I overheard her one night, talking on the phone. She'd found out that I wasn't living off of Pop's money. She wasn't interested in me, just my money," he shrugged. "It's been a recurring problem I've had for years. First, people assume Pop is leaving a chunk of his estate to me. And then they find out about my own success. If I ever meet someone not out for just the money, I'll think about it."

Jack sat down at the table and started eating. She

poured herself a fresh cup of coffee and sat down across from him, pushing the food around on her plate.

Jack leaned back in his chair and studied her pale features. "I've had my friend who has the security and PI firm to do some digging on your parents."

"What kind of digging?" she pushed her plate away. She had managed to take a couple of bites of the omelet but she just didn't have an appetite this morning.

"After you found that letter, I asked him if he could find out anything about who your mom might have been leaving town with, or even who your biological dad might be."

"It's been over fifteen years. How would they be able to find who she was leaving with, if the police couldn't?"

"To the police, they had a murder-suicide on their hands, and they didn't care about why it went down. As long as it wasn't a homicide, it didn't matter to them," Jack shrugged. "I, uh, went through some more of those boxes Helen kept for you and found some journals your mom wrote. You should read them sometime."

"What's in them?"

"Everything she never said to you and should have, for one thing. And the name of your biological father." Jack stared across the table at her, watching as her already pale face drained of every bit of color. "Hell, I'm sorry. I shouldn't have told you that, not today, anyway."

"No, it's okay," Nicole reached across the table and patted his arm. "It's just, it's still hard to wrap my head around it all, you know?" she shook her head. "For over thirty years, I've thought of one man as my father and that my mother hated me. In the space of a few months, I've learned she didn't hate me, but he's not my father. Add that in with my bastard of a fiancé cheated on me with someone else, well, today is just starting out to be a shitty day."

Making a sound of agreement, Jack stacked the plates, getting ready to clear the table. "So, what do you want to do? Brian is more than happy to at least run the name your mom put in her journal. Brian is former military, too. If the guy wasn't just blowing smoke up your mom's ass and really was stationed at Hood, he'll find him for you."

Nicole stared into her coffee cup for a moment. "I need to think that one through. It wouldn't just be my life changing with that knowledge.

"Fair enough."

She gave him a sad smile. "I would like those journals, if you have them handy."

"Of course. I'll go grab them for you. I only found four, but from the way they're written, I think if you looked through everything Ma has in that barn, you might find more of them," he set the dirty plates in the sink and wiped his hands on a towel. "Are you going back to your condo this morning, or what?"

"No, I think I'm going to head out. Thanks, Jack. You can be pretty nice, when you want to be." She gave him a watery smile and finished her coffee, standing up to put the cup in the sink.

"Yeah, if I had a dollar for every time a woman told me that," Jack shot her a grin.

"You'd have a dollar," she teased, crossing over to him and placing a soft kiss on his cheek. "I'll clean up the kitchen for you."

"No need. I'm going to work from home today. I'll get it

done," he turned her and gave her a gentle push in the direction of her room. "Go get your stuff together and I'll go grab those journals for you."

It didn't take her long to get her stuff back together. She met Jack back out in the kitchen and he pointed to the journals stacked on the table. "Did you read all of them?"

"Yes, well, more like skimmed them. I wasn't sure if you'd want them or not, and I wanted to try and give Brian as much as I could to go on," he explained as she picked the books up. He grabbed the handle of her suitcase and walked her out to her car.

"Be careful driving."

"I'll be careful," Nicole promised as she rolled her eyes. "And I'll call when I get to the hotel," she tacked on before he could mention it.

"And take lots of notes for me, if you wind up going to the conference," he held her door open for her, shutting it once she was behind the wheel. She hit the button to lower the window.

"Thanks, Jack. I owe you one."

"You owe me more than one. Now, get out of here," he tapped the roof of her car and stepped back, allowing her to start it and drive away.

Nicole had no idea what she was going to do next, but first she'd get to San Antonio and decompress. Then maybe she could take some time to figure out what to do with this mess.

CHAPTER 27

Nicole arrived in san antonio before the allowed check-in time at the hotel, so she decided to spend the time walking around the River Walk. It had been years since she had been in San Antonio, and she was curious to see the changes. She walked along the waterway, watching the boats of tourists drift by, enjoying the enticing aromas from the many restaurants.

She found herself exiting the Riverwalk near The Alamo, the doomed mission in the heart of the city where the fight for Texas' independence had begun. Although she had been there countless times before, it had been a few years and she decided to enter the shrine. It was always fun to listen to the tour guides tell the stories of The Alamo. And of course, they never failed to mention the rumors of the gold that was supposed to be buried somewhere on the grounds.

It was after three o'clock before she made her way back to her hotel, stopping in the garage to grab her bag out of the trunk of her car. She tossed the key card and her purse on the desk, and stowed the bag in the closet, and then stretched out on the bed. Her eyes were starting to burn, from the lack of sleep and the number of tears she'd shed the night before over Jason.

Oh God. Jason. She still couldn't believe what was happening to her. She had trusted him, had given him her love, and now it looked like he'd played her for the fool. Maybe her mother had been right all along. Maybe it was better to not trust, to not love. Maybe it was better to live out your life alone, live for yourself and not anyone else.

She turned on her side, curling up into a ball, and cried, feeling her heart break into ten thousand pieces, all over again.

After the tears stopped, she forced herself to get up and call Jack to let him know she had made it to San Antonio without any difficulty. They talked about the conference for a few minutes and she assured him she was planning on attending at least a couple of the workshops.

"I don't care about that, Nicole. I'm just worried about you," he told her. "We all are," he added after a brief hesitation.

"Has he been by your place?" she asked with a slight catch in her voice. If Jack heard it, he didn't comment.

"Yeah, a couple of hours ago now. He's pretty upset, Nicole. He swears it's all just a misunderstanding, and he needs to talk to you."

"A misunderstanding? He was in the shower and she was in his room, answering the phone!" She heard her voice escalating, and struggled to regain her composure.

"Don't shoot the messenger. I'm just saying that once you are ready to listen, he wants to talk to you. He left here to go over to the ranch to talk to Mitch and Carly. And don't worry, Carly isn't going to give him any information, although she might give him a few bruises." Jack assured her.

"Sorry. I'm tired and feel like my life has gone from sugar to shit in the blink of an eye," she apologized. "I think I'm going to grab a nap and then head to this dinner workshop tonight. I'll call you sometime tomorrow."

"It's all good. I remember a time or two where I told you to 'fuck off' when I was in that VA hospital," he told her with a chuckle.

"You threw a few things at me, too. Good thing your aim sucks," Nicole shot back with a laugh. "Thanks, Jack."

"You know I've always got your back."

Nicole disconnected the call and retrieved one of her mother's journals from her bag. Stretching out on the bed, she skimmed through it, promising herself she'd go back and read it in more detail later.

Jack was right, it was full of all the praise and feelings of love Nicole would have loved to have heard as a child and teenager. Every one of her accomplishments was in all capital letters or underlined or starred. Even the little things like her perfect attendance were noted.

And it detailed how her mother was afraid of telling Nicole how she felt. Her mother had always been afraid of the bottom falling out of her world, just like Nicole was. Her mother had suffered through so many disappointments in life, she didn't know how to look for the good.

The journal she'd picked up didn't cover the years before her parents were married or mention who her biological father was. It did talk about how the man she thought of as her father was always doing little things for her mom and how her mom felt guilty for not having the same depth of emotion for him. Her mother had loved her dad, just hadn't been in love with him.

Nicole set the book aside and rolled onto her side, a tear sliding down her cheek. She and her mother were so much alike, it seemed. What a shame that they couldn't talk about this, then or now. Closing her eyes, Nicole cried for the first time for the mother she'd lost.

AFTER A SHORT NAP, Nicole forced herself to get up so she could attend the dinner workshop. It would make her focus on something other than her own problems, at least for a few hours. She ran into a few former classmates and found herself agreeing to a night out on the town with them, delaying her return to an empty hotel room for as long as possible. But when it became obvious her associates were planning on hitting as many bars as they could on the Riverwalk, she begged off and made her way back to the hotel.

She told herself she wasn't disappointed that Jason hadn't called her cell phone all day. She told herself she was strong and she would survive this heartbreak, too. As she sank down onto the bed, she admitted to herself she was a liar.

CHAPTER 28

Nicole tossed and turned all night, deciding to give up around six o'clock. She ordered breakfast from room service, sitting by the window to eat, lost in thought.

Jack had given her a lot to think about yesterday. Did she want to find her birth father? And if she did, what then? How do you show up on someone's doorstep, thirty something years later, and announce that their one night stand resulted in you? There were a thousand questions running through her brain that she wanted answers to. But there were a thousand and one reasons why she should let it drop.

Maybe she should just contact Jack's friend herself, see what he had to say, what the process would entail. There was nothing wrong with being armed with information, right?

Finishing with her breakfast, she stepped into the bathroom and took a hot shower, her thoughts still centered on the possibility of finding this stranger. Maybe she could skip the conference and go read those journals. Jack had said the name was in one of them, hadn't he?

As she stepped out of the shower, she heard the phone in the bedroom ring, and she hurried to answer it. "Hello?"

"Hi. It's me," Jason's voice sounded in her ear. "Please don't hang up." She bit her lip and tightened her grip on the phone, his voice stopping her from doing just that. His voice was so soft with just a touch of pleading in it. "Nicole?"

"I'm here," she answered on a sigh. "How did you know where to find me?"

"I knew Jack was supposed to be at that conference this weekend, so when he was still in Waketon and you weren't, I took a chance. I started calling the hotels in San Antonio and asked for you until one of them transferred me to your room," he admitted. "I need to talk to you. Have breakfast with me," he pleaded.

"Jason," she sighed, closing her eyes.

"Please."

"You're four hours away," she stalled.

"I'm in a coffee shop downtown where I've spent the last hour dialing twenty hotels looking for you," he countered. "Baby, we need to talk," his voice was low, insistent.

"I need my head examined," she muttered.

"What was that?"

"Nothing," she gave in, knowing she needed to see him. They needed to resolve this and either move on together or let it be the end.

"Meet me in forty-five minutes at the Starbucks on the South end of the River Walk," she instructed before hanging up the receiver, not even waiting for his answer.

Her hair and make-up needed to be perfect for this meeting. No way was she going to let him know she'd been up all night crying over him.

Forty-five minutes after hanging up the phone, she stepped into the coffee shop. He was already there waiting for her. His eyes lit up when he saw her, standing up to hold a chair for her at the table he had grabbed. Bending his head to kiss her, she turned her head to one side, allowing him to kiss her cheek.

"I ordered you a latte," he indicated the cup on the table in front of her.

"You said you wanted to talk," she reminded him, taking a sip of the coffee for a lack of anything better to do.

He reached across the table for her hand but she pulled away, placing both hands in her lap. With a heavy sigh, Jason's eyes searched hers. "Are you going to listen to what I have to say?"

"I'll listen," she agreed.

"I know it sounded bad the other night, but nothing happened between Sara and me, I swear," he told her. "I didn't know she was going to be at the conference. I ran into my friend Matt that first day. Sara found us during one of the breaks and invited herself to dinner with me and Matt. Matt is too nice of a guy to tell her 'no', and I think he's always had a thing for her. Anyway, I spent the evening talking to Matt, catching up. The only conversations I had with Sara revolved around you. I told her all about you."

"What did you tell her?" she fiddled with the insulator on her cup.

"I told her how much I love you. I told her how smart

241

you are, how you make me laugh…" his voice trailed off. "I told her I was looking forward to spending the rest of my life with you."

"Why didn't you tell me you'd run into her?" she couldn't keep the hurt out of her voice.

"Because to me it was nothing! I love *you*. I'm marrying *you*," he paused as she raised her eyebrow.

"Then why was she in your room at ten o'clock at night, while you were in the shower?" her voice was rising so she clamped her mouth shut, gritting her teeth.

"She wasn't there by invitation. She got one of the desk clerks to let her into my room. Hotel management is dealing with that issue." he leaned forward, bracing his arms on the table. "Baby, I swear to you, I didn't encourage her. She knew as soon as I said your name who I meant. Her jealousy of you was always an issue between us."

He paused, his eyes never leaving her face. "I heard the phone ringing and I heard her answer it. I walked out of the bathroom and found her draped across the bed in…well, that part doesn't matter. I pulled her off the bed and shoved her into the hall with her screaming obscenities at me," his lips twitched as he remembered the scene.

"The hotel's management had a few words with me about my 'ungentlemanly' conduct. They backed down pretty quick when I said my fiancé is an attorney and I was thinking of suing them for allowing an unauthorized person to have access to my room." He again reached for her hand. This time, Nicole allowed him to take her hand in his.

"Tell me you believe me," he implored, his fingers tightening around hers, his eyes catching and holding hers.

"I...I want to, Jason. I do," she sighed and closed her eyes. "But I need time to think."

"Look at me, Cole." he waited for her eyes to open. "In all honesty, do you think I would cheat on you?"

She looked down at their joined hands, and then back up, into his eyes. The worry was there for her to see and the panic that he was going to lose her, if he hadn't already.

What was it Mitch had said to her so many weeks ago? She could either learn from her mistakes or wallow in self-pity and blame everyone else, like her mother had done. She thought back to the conversation she'd had with Jack yesterday morning. She could be like him and let the bitterness rule her life for a while.

It all came down to trust.

She turned her head and looked out at the river, studying the people walking by, many of them couples walking hand in hand. His thumb was rubbing across her knuckles, offering his strength and comfort the only way he could right now. She could feel the intensity of his gaze on her.

She had walked away from this man once before, and had spent years being alone because of her own fears and insecurities. The Fates had given them a second chance, and her heart was telling her, begging her to take it.

She turned her hand in his, her fingers lacing with his. "No, you're not the type to cheat," she answered, her voice soft but without a shred of doubt in it.

Releasing the breath he'd been holding, his grip on her hand tightening as he brought her hand to his mouth, brushing a kiss across her knuckles.

"Did I lose you?" he whispered.

"You came pretty damn close," she admitted as she blinked away her tears.

"I was so afraid you had run off again," he admitted, his eyes caressing her face.

She shook her head, "No, I'm through with running. I just needed some space. I would have come back and had it out with you. It means a lot to me that you came after me though."

"I've learned from my mistakes, too," he acknowledged. "But you can't keep running out on me every time we have a fight," he teased, squeezing her hand.

"Then don't get caught in hotel rooms with half-naked women!" she shot back, squeezing his hand in return.

"Never again, from now on, we both go to those damn things." he promised.

"Oh, that'll be fun. I'll get to sit in a hotel room while you're off learning about doctor stuff. Yippee." she drawled, rolling her eyes. "Are you going to come to the legal seminars and workshops with me?"

"No, we'll make Jack go to those," he grinned across the table at her. "Are you ready to go?" he motioned towards her coffee cup and she nodded. They walked out of the shop and she led the way back to her hotel.

"Where do we go next?" he asked as they entered her room. She tossed her purse on the table and turned to him.

"I'm supposed to be attending a conference," she reminded him, raising an eyebrow as he moved across the room towards her, his hands going to the buttons on his shirt.

"So am I, but instead I'm chasing my fiancé all over the state of Texas," he pulled his shirt off and reached for her, helping her off with her own shirt. He bent and swung her up in his arms, laying her in the middle of the bed, stretching out beside her. He leaned over and kissed her eyes closed before kissing her lips and spreading kisses down her neck.

She wrapped her arms around him, not even aware of the tears rolling down her cheeks until Jason felt them. He levered himself up onto his elbows, wiping the tears away, murmuring soothing words to her.

"Honey, what's wrong?" he pulled her into his arms and shifted so that he was on his back and her head was pillowed on his chest.

She sniffled a few times and lifted her head so he could see her face. "Nothing's wrong. For the first time in a very long time, I feel like everything is finally right."

He wiped the last few tears from her cheeks with his thumbs, bending his head to press soft kisses to her forehead, eyes, cheeks, and then her lips.

"Are you still going to marry me in six weeks?" he asked in-between kisses. His lips moved to her neck.

"Might as well," she teased, tilting her head to give him better access to the pulse points along her neck.

"Might as well?" he pulled back to give her a mock frown.

"I do already have my dress," she told him. "And we have the church reserved and Aunt Helen is planning that huge party for us."

"All of those are good reasons to have the wedding," Jason agreed, his fingers stroking her waist.

"And you, Mitch, and Jack all have your tuxes ordered."

"This is true," he agreed, his fingers sliding over her

skin, stroking just below her breasts. "You're very vulnerable, here. You shouldn't tease me about our wedding."

He bent his head and sucked on her nipple. Her back arched and she moaned, encouraging him to do more. "Should I stop?" he asked, lifting his head.

"No, don't stop!" she reached for him, trying to pull him back down to her.

"So I can do more of this?" he asked, switching to her other breast.

"Oh, God, yes!" she cried out, her nails digging into his shoulders. "Jason, please?"

"Please what, baby?" he undid the button her jeans and lowered the zipper. His fingers eased under the band of her underwear.

"Just...love me!" she cried, her back arching again.

"Oh, I do, babe. Believe me, I do," he raised himself up, giving her a hard kiss before standing up.

Bewildered by physical withdrawal, she opened her eyes. "What...Oh!" she cried out as he dragged her pants and underwear down her legs and off.

"This time it's going to be rough and fast," he warned her as he climbed back onto the bed and positioned himself between her legs.

"As long as there's a next time," she agreed on a sigh as he slid into her, her arms wrapping around him and holding on tight.

LATER THAT AFTERNOON, Nicole showed Jason the journals Jack had given her and gave him a brief rundown of what Jack had told her the day before.

"You never knew your mom kept a journal?" he asked, flipping through the pages.

"To be honest, I didn't pay any attention. There was so much tension between us, I avoided her as much as possible," Nicole shrugged her shoulders. "Jack says there are others."

"Did you read these yet?" Jason looked at the four journals spread out between them.

"I skimmed through one of them," she ran a finger along the edge of one of the bindings. "If I decide to try and find him..." she had to stop and swallow hard.

"Your birth dad?" he asked when she didn't continue.

"Yeah, *that* him," she looked up at him. "I'm at a loss as to what to call him, either of them now. All my life, there's been just one man I've thought of as my dad. Now I find out there's someone else out there I should have been calling that."

"That one man will always be your dad. No matter what he did, or why, or how angry you are at him, he was the one there for you for those first fifteen years," he pointed out. "This other guy, right now, he's just an unknown sperm donor. Granted, we have no idea what he did after that night with your mom. But he wasn't around when you needed him."

"Do you think I should find him?" her fingers played with a fold on the bedspread.

"I can't tell you what to do here, babe. But I will support you, whatever you decide."

"I know. It'd be a hell of a lot easier if you could just tell me, though," she admitted on a sigh. His picked up the journals and set them on the nightstand before stretching out. Reaching out, he took her hand and pulled her across the small space separating them until she was lying across his chest.

"Okay, so let's talk this out. Just say whatever first comes into your mind. No wrong or right, no judging. Just say it. Ready?" Jason wrapped his arms around her, holding her against him.

Nicole shifted until her head was on his shoulder and took a slow, deep breath before nodding. "Ready."

"Do you want to know his name?"

"Yes," Nicole answered without hesitation.

"So we read the journals. That one was easy," his arm tightened around her in a gentle squeeze. "Next up, do you want to find him?"

"I want to know where he is but not have to talk to him yet." That answer was a little slower to come, but she still said it with conviction.

"Do you want him to be at our wedding, if we find him before then?"

"No." Nicole looked up at him with a frown. "Why would you ask that?"

"Because it establishes a timeline for you. We're getting married in six weeks and if you want him there, then we need to hire this guy Jack knows and find him fast." Jason cupped her cheek with his palm. "If you want to sit on it, think about it more, we can do that, too."

Nicole nodded her understanding. "I need to read the journals before I decide anything."

"Then you have your answer. At least part of it. Read her journals and see how you feel after that," he nudged her chin up with his knuckles so he could look in her eyes.

"And know that you are not going through any of this alone."

"Sounds like I have a plan," Nicole yawned. "I think I need a nap."

"Then go to sleep, baby," he pressed a kiss to her forehead. "We'll paint the town after you wake up."

Nicole nodded, her eyes already drifting closed. She was back in his arms and they had their plans. With any luck, nothing else would happen to derail them.

CHAPTER 29

"Home, sweet home." Jason told her as he unlocked the door to their condo. Nicole smiled at him and stepped inside. They'd had to drive home in separate cars, since they'd both driven to San Antonio.

"Thanks for staying in San Antonio with me."

"We needed the time together." He carried the bags in and set them down next to her, leaning in to kiss her. "And you needed me."

"I do need you. But I still feel bad you missed most of your conference," her arms went around his waist and she pulled him closer.

"I saw what I wanted to see that first day. And you are much more important than any conference," he pushed her up against the wall.

"Want to go take a nap?" he wiggled his eyebrows, just as her phone rang from her pocket.

"Don't answer it," he implored, as she retrieved it.

"It's Aunt Helen. If I don't answer, she'll just come over," she warned him as she accepted the call.

"Hi Aunt Helen," she said into the phone, smothering her own laugh at Jason's disgruntled look. She pushed against his shoulder to make him step back and let her go. He brushed one last kiss against her cheek before he turned to go her bags out of her car.

"No, we just walked in the door. Jason's getting all the bags in now." she answered her aunt as she watched him walk away. With a sigh, she turned her attention back to her phone call.

"I promise, everything is fine, Aunt Helen. We took some time to be with each other and talk about some other stuff going on," Nicole rolled her eyes as Jason came back through the front door. He tossed a smirk her way and carried her bags into the bedroom. She headed over to the couch and settled back for what was bound to be a long conversation, prepared to update her aunt on what she'd decided to do with the wedding and her search for her birth father.

AFTER TAKING their bags to the bedroom, Jason decided to hang out in there for a while, guessing that Nicole would want to talk to her aunt about the journals and some of the information in them. Realizing he couldn't hear the muffled sound of her voice any longer, Jason went in search of his fiancé, finding her out on the deck, staring down at the lake. He stepped up behind her, wrapping his arms around her waist. Nicole leaned back against him and sighed.

"You okay?" he questioned, his mouth next to her ear.

"I'm fine," she assured him, turning her head just enough to give him a kiss. "Just enjoying the view out here. I'll miss this deck when we move in a few months."

"What did Helen need?"

"She wanted to sure we made it back home without any problems," she glanced at him. "And that we're okay."

His arms tightened around her as he pulled her in even closer. "What did you tell her?"

"I told her that we were still getting married in a few weeks, seeing as how she and Carly already have everything planned out for us...Jason!" she squealed as he bent and picked her up, tossing her over his shoulder as he turned back to the condo to head inside.

"I warned you about teasing me," he laughed as she squirmed, trying to get him to put her down.

"Please, I'm sorry. No more teasing..." she managed to choke out through her laughter as he carried her through the condo to their bedroom. He stopped at the foot of the bed and leaned over, letting her drop onto the mattress. With his hands on either side of her, he trapped her on the bed.

"Now, what was that about getting married?"

Pressing her lips together to make herself stop laughing, Nicole swallowed. "I told her we are fine, we're getting married in six weeks, and that I'd talk to her tomorrow."

"Tomorrow, huh? I figured she'd be busting down the door by now, needing you to look at more bridal stuff," he shuddered.

"It hasn't been that bad!" she giggled again. "And I told her that I was tired, after going to the conference and then having to drive back up here."

"Oh, well, if you're tired, I should let you sleep..." he moved to push away from her, chuckling as she grabbed him by his belt loops and pulled him down on top of her.

"Oh, no, you don't. We had make-up sex at the hotel, now it's time for 'welcome home sex'!" she told him as her hands went to work on his belt. With a delighted laugh, he went to work on getting her clothes off of her as well.

"I really like the way you think, baby!" He told her, rolling them over so that she was straddling him. "You do realize welcome home sex may take hours, right?"

"I'm counting on it," she whispered, leaning over him to kiss him, gasping in pleasure as his hands moved over her. She adjusted her position, feeling him pressing against her, seeking entrance.

"God, I love the way you feel!" he groaned as he slid inside of her.

"Feeling's mutual!" she managed to gasp as his hips began to thrust up into her. "Now shut up and make love to me!" she demanded, leaning over to kiss him.

"Yes, ma'am!"

"WELL, look what the cat dragged in!" Mitch greeted them as Nicole and Jason entered the dining room at the ranch the next day.

"Where's Aunt Helen?" Nicole asked, ignoring her cousin and accepting the cup of coffee Carly poured and held out to her.

"In the kitchen, with Steve," Carly told her, pouring another cup for Jason. "Do you have time to go over some of the details for your wedding while you're both here?"

"After I talk to Aunt Helen," Nicole promised.

"Do you want me to come with you?" he asked her, leaning over to kiss her cheek

"No, you stay here and catch up with Carly and Mitch. I'm sure Carly has all kinds of questions for us that you can answer for her," Nicole bit her lip to keep from laughing at Jason's pained look.

"Minx," he muttered as he turned back to the table. "Any food left?"

Nicole shook her head, a smile on her face, as she walked down the hall to the kitchen to find her aunt and uncle.

"Good morning, sweetheart! What brings you over so early?" Helen greeted her as she stepped into the kitchen.

"I wanted to talk to you guys." Nicole moved over to the table and slid into one of the kitchen chairs. She'd brought the journals with her and she set them down on the table.

"Did you know my mother kept journals?" she asked her aunt.

Helen glanced at the notebooks and nodded. "I figured they were in those boxes somewhere," she looked at her niece. "Your mom and I were so different, and she didn't confide in me. I thought if she wanted me to know her secrets, she would have just told me. I never thought about you wanting to know more."

"If Jason and I hadn't gotten back together, I'm not sure I would want to know more," Nicole admitted. Her grip tightened on her coffee cup. "Did you know Dad wasn't my real dad?"

A look passed between Helen and Steve.

"You knew?" Nicole looked between them.

"We *guessed*," Steve corrected with a sigh. "Your mother wanted out of this town and away from this kind of life. I offered to loan her the money to go to college, but that woman was proud. She wasn't going unless she could make it on her own," he paused to take a sip of his own coffee.

"She and a couple of her friends would go over to Austin and spend the weekend, partying. And then all of a sudden, that stopped. And then she announced she and your dad were getting married. It wasn't long after that, she told me she was pregnant," Helen picked up the story. "She was excited, but there was sadness there, too. But she wouldn't talk to me about it."

"And your dad, he said they'd been dating for a while, but had kept it secret because he was older and didn't want people to think bad of her," Steve added.

"He loved her, and in her way, she loved him. Her love just wasn't as deep as his was," Helen assured her as she glanced down at the journals again. "What do the journals say?"

"She met a young soldier from Ft. Hood in Austin on one of her weekend trips. She names him in this one," Nicole reached over and tapped on the top journal with a fingernail. "But I don't think she ever tried to find him. I think...I think I want to try."

Helen and Steve both nodded. "We'll help in any way we can."

"I know. Jack knows someone who we can hire. I'm not going to worry about it until after the wedding, though. We also might see if he can find out any information on who she was leaving with that day, why dad snapped like he did."

Steve reached over and patted her hand. "He loved her, Nicole. And he loved you. Whatever else you find out, never doubt that."

"I know. And I know mom was the way she was because of everything that had ever happened to her. But he robbed me of the chance to ever fix things between us. She wasn't an angel, but he wasn't a saint either, I guess."

Helen gave her niece a sympathetic look. "But now you have Jason, and a chance for everything your dad ever wanted for you. Hold onto that, Nicole," she, too, reached over to lay her hand on top of Nicole's. "I'd like to read the journals, when you're done. I should have read those years ago."

Nicole smiled at her aunt and uncle. "Thank you, both of you, for everything you have done for me. I hope you know how much you mean to me."

"We do, honey. And you mean just as much to us," Steve told her, his voice gruff.

"Now, about that wedding..." Nicole smiled, ready to change the subject. Helen launched into plans for the reception and Steve pushed back his chair, making comments about needing to find Mitch and getting to work. Jason was not the only one with an aversion to these details, it would seem.

CHAPTER 30

S ix weeks later, nicole stood alone in the Bride's
Room at the church, staring at her reflection in the
mirror. She heard the door open, and she looked
over to see her aunt, standing in the doorway.

"Oh, honey, you are so beautiful!" Helen stepped over
and pressed her cheek to Nicole's. "I'm sorry your parents
aren't here to see this." She adjusted the fall of the veil and
fluffed her dress a little.

"I am too, a little. I wish Daddy were here to walk me
down the aisle," Nicole's eyes met her aunt's in the mirror.

"Thank you for everything you've done, both this
summer as well as the past fifteen years." She wrapped her
arm around her aunt and they stood, looking at their reflection in the mirror.

"I wish your mother had confided in me. I'd have
supported her when she found out she was pregnant with
you. Maybe Steve and I could have found your birth father
for her. But she couldn't see past the mess of Jack's mom.
And she was scared, for you as well as herself. But she

never got to experience true love was," Helen turned to her niece, clasping both of her hands in her own. "And that was her loss, not to experience what you and Jason share. Don't ever let that hold you back again. You deserve every bit of happiness that man wants to give you."

Nicole's eyes filled with tears as she nodded at her aunt.

"Hey you two no more mushy stuff," Carly stepped into the room and handed Nicole her bouquet. "You'll ruin your makeup!"

The three women stood side by side, looking at their reflection. "We sure do make this family look good, don't we?" Carly joked, causing the other Nicole to giggle. "They're about ready for us. Jack's on his way up. Are you ready to do this?" Carly asked, smiling at her friend.

Nicole smiled back. "I've been ready." She glanced over at her aunt. "Why don't you go let the usher seat you now?"

Jack was stepping into the room as Helen reached the door. As she passed by him, he leaned down to kiss her cheek. Carly gave Nicole one last smile and followed Helen out the door, leaving Jack and Nicole alone.

"Hey, kid. How are you holding up?" he stepped over to stand in front of her.

"I'm fine. How are the guys?" She reached up to straighten his bowtie. Mitch and Jason had tried to outdrink Jack the night before at the bachelor party, but had forgotten to make Jack drink something other than whiskey. So while they were struggling with the hangovers from hell today, he was his usual chipper self.

"We poured enough coffee into them that they're somewhat sober. At least they didn't scream in agony when we forced them to remove their sunglasses." Jack chuckled and offered her his arm as they left the room and moved to the stairwell.

The doors to the chapel were closed, the ushers at the ready to open them once The Wedding March started to play. Jack laid his hand over hers where it rested on his forearm.

"This is it, kiddo; one last chance to run screaming in the other direction." Jack jerked his head towards the front door, and she smiled up at him.

"No, thanks, I'm ready to spend the rest of my life with the one I love." Her brilliant smile spoke volumes. Jack gave her hand one last squeeze as the opening strains of The Wedding March played, and the ushers opened the doors. She was aware of the packed church as she and Jack walked down the aisle, but her attention was on Jason, as his was on hers.

All of the butterflies in her stomach settled down as their eyes met. The love in his eyes was there for everyone to see. There were times she still pinched herself to make sure she wasn't dreaming, but this was the real deal. He was her life now and she was his.

Jack paused to kiss her cheek when they reached the alter. "Be happy, little one," he whispered, handing her over to Jason. Jason took her hand and looked down into her eyes as the minister started to speak the old familiar words.

She wouldn't remember what prayers the minister said, or the verses he read, but she'd never forget the pure love that was shining out of Jason's eyes as he held her hand and promised to love, honor and cherish her for the rest of their lives. She cried as he slipped the diamond studded wedding band on her ring finger.

"I now pronounce you husband and wife." The minister proclaimed as he took her in his arms for their first kiss as husband and wife.

"You are so beautiful. I love you," he murmured as he held her close. They turned towards their family and friends, who erupted into applause and cheers as they made their way back down the aisle.

It took an eternity for the church to empty and the photographer to finish with the shots of the wedding party and family. Jason helped her into the limo for the ride out to the ranch and the reception, climbing in after her wrapping his arms around her once the door was closed.

"Hello, wife," he whispered, bending his head for a kiss.

"Hello, husband," she whispered back, tucking her head against his shoulder as the car started moving. "How's the head?"

"Damn that Jack and his whiskey. How can that man drink as much, if not more, than Mitch and I did and still walk around as if nothing was wrong?"

"Something about his metabolism, he told me once. He never suffers a hangover." She informed him, laughing. "At least he stuck around to sober you up in time for the wedding."

He grinned down at her and leaned his head back against the seat of the limo. "How long do we need to stay at the reception?"

"Dinner, toasts, cake and dancing, I'd say a couple of hours, at least." She looked up at him. "Why?"

"I'm looking forward to helping you out of this dress." He fingered the lace of her bodice and grinned down at her. "I can tell the driver to take the long way..." slapping at his fingers, Nicole laughed.

"Uh-huh. I've been too nervous to eat today, and I'm hungry! Besides, the sooner we get there, the sooner we can leave for our private honeymoon."

"Nervous, what did you have to be nervous about? I was the one standing up at the front of the church looking at a set of closed doors, wondering if you were ever going to step through them," he teased, wrapping his arm around her shoulders and keeping her close to his side as the limo started down the long driveway to the ranch house.

"And I was nervous because I saw Mitch when he stumbled home this morning. As bad as he looked, I was sure you looked worse and would ruin my wedding pictures. You two should have known better than to get drunk with Jack." She elbowed him in the ribs as the car coasted to a stop in front of the ranch house.

The ranch hands had helped construct an arch and trellis, and laid out a red carpet for everyone to walk from the driveway around to the backyard for the reception. The guests were already lined up, awaiting their arrival.

Jack stepped to the microphone on the bandstand that been erected for the occasion as Jason helped her climbed out of the limo. "Ladies and Gentlemen, please help me welcome the guests of honor, Jason and Nicole Morrow!" Mitch and Carly handed glasses of champagne over to them as everyone raised their glasses in a toast.

They made their way through the crowd of people to the head table and took their seats, flanked by family and friends. Mitch and Carly had served as best man and matron of honor, and three of the doctors Jason worked with had served as the ushers. The band was playing in the background, while the caterers' staff moved among the tables, serving drinks and bringing out the food.

Her estimation, and his hope, of having to stay at the reception for only a couple of hours proved correct. After they ate their dinner, they began to circulate around the tables. They danced their first dance and listened to the toasts made by Mitch, Carly and Jack.

As soon as they'd cut the cake and fed it to each other, Jason pulled Nicole up on stage and over to the microphone. "All right, y'all. I hope you are all having fun, but Nicole and I are going to be leaving now. Y'all are welcome to stay and enjoy Helen and Steve's hospitality, but we will see you in two weeks. If you try looking for us before then, you'd better be ready to run!" He swung her up in his arms and, with Mitch and Jack leading the way, carried her back out to the limo.

"If you want to toss the bouquet, darlin', you'd better do it!" Jason instructed as he waited for the driver to open the door.

She grinned up at him and turned herself in his arms so that her back was to the crowd and tossed her bouquet over his shoulder, turning to see one of the nurses from the hospital catch it. Her date turned red in the face, as the doctors near them started teasing the couple.

She paused before getting into the limo to kiss her family one last time and then he was urging her into the limo and climbing in behind her. The driver shut the door on them and hurried around to the driver's side.

"Whew!" he grinned down at her. "What a day!" he wrapped his arm around her shoulders. "I'm ready for a vacation, how about you?"

"I'd like to know where we're going," she snuggled close.

"The Bahamas." He played with one of her curls, sending shivers down her spine. "We leave first thing in the morning. Tonight, we're staying at a hotel in Austin, near the airport," he nuzzled her neck with his lips.

"Jason..." she leaned back from him and looked pointedly at the privacy window.

"Spoilsport," he laughed and pulled her back into his arms. "Relax. He's taking us over to the airport and we're catching the commuter flight to Austin. We fly to the Bahamas tomorrow morning," wrapping his arms around her, he pulled her in closer to him. "I missed having you in the condo this week. I still can't believe Helen made you move back to the ranch."

"Be grateful it was only for the week. She made Mitch and Carly split up for the month preceding their wedding." Carly had reminded her and Helen of that fact many times over the last month.

"I missed you, too." she admitted. "Thank you."

"For what?" he looked down at her in puzzlement.

"For giving me my happily ever after," Nicole told him with a grin as she slipped a hand around his neck and tugged his mouth back down to hers. Just before he claimed her lips again, Jason whispered a single word to her.

"Always."

ABOUT THE AUTHOR

Kelli grew up all over the East Coast but her family finally settled in Cincinnati long enough for her to finish high school and college. She has always loved to read books and write her own stories. In high school, she used to pass around the latest chapter of the story she was writing for her friends to read. There is more than one high school teacher out there that can probably remember telling her to put the book down and pay attention to the lectures.

Graduating from the University of Cincinnati with her BS in Nursing, she left Ohio for Texas and the U.S. Army. She received a medical discharge for a knee injury, but was able to meet the man she'd one day call her husband first-- thanks to some mutual friends who insisted they would be perfect together. And what do you know--they are!

She continued to read books by the dozens and write her own stories. And then one day, a friend dared her to enter a contest. She didn't win, but the feedback she received from the judges convinced her that maybe people were interested in the stories she wanted to tell. She still lives in Central Texas, with her husband, two children and 2 dogs.

www.ingramcontent.com/pod-product-compliance
Lightning Source LLC
Chambersburg PA
CBHW020311200626
46814CB00006BA/2186